MIRANDA ELAINE

Editor: Emily A. Lawrence with Lawrence Editing
Proofreading: Julie Deaton of Deaton Author Services
Cover Designer: Jay Aheer with Simply Defined Art
Photo Credit: Lindee Robinson Photography
Interior Design and Formatting: Stacey Blake of Champagne Book Design

For Megan.

Your never-ending positivity and encouragement is the breath of fresh air we all need in our lives. I absolutely couldn't have written this book without you or all of the purple. You inspire me every day and I strive to live my best life just like you. Please never change. You. Are. Perfect.

CHAPTER 1

Leni

"LENI, YOU IN HERE?" A BOOMING VOICE BREAKS ME OUT of my fantasy world. It's the same voice that's been forcing my head out of books and making me live in the real world for the last eighteen years.

It's Griffin Thorne, my best friend, and the only person other than Nan who's able to call me out on my bullshit and survive. Though it hasn't always been that way. Once upon a time, he was my worst enemy. Luckily, we got over that because now I can't fathom my life without him.

"Reading," I call out in warning. He should know by now that interrupting me in the middle of a good book does not come without some sort of retaliation.

"No, no, no!" He storms into my bedroom and stares down at me cuddled up in the middle of my giant, gray bean-bag chair. I got it from my nan for my birthday last year. It's huge and soft and perfect for an afternoon with my latest book obsession.

"It's noon on a Saturday and last week you promised me you'd go to the cookout with me today. It's the first one Shelby and Jack have had since the baby was born." He walks across my crowded room, stepping over several piles of books to glare down at me. "The whole firehouse is coming to celebrate. Now up and at 'em. The fictional world can wait, the real world is calling."

1

He's annoyed with me. I don't blame him. He's a social person by nature and I'm perfectly content to only hang out with him and Nan.

"Ugh, seriously? People, public, and nature? All in one day? What did I ever do to you to deserve such a harsh punishment?" Without as much as moving my book, I pull the lightweight pink crocheted blanket currently on my lap over my head, attempting to hide from this cruel world.

"You bailed on our hike last week. You owe me." His stern expression isn't fading. I was hoping he'd forget, not that Griffin Thorne has ever forgotten anything. I swear he has the memory of an elephant; I can barely remember what I had for breakfast yesterday and he could tell me what I wore on the first day of tenth grade if I asked him.

I peek through the blanket over my head. He's not budging. He's definitely not letting me out of today.

"Fine!" I pout as I pull the blanket off of the top of my head and into my lap. "Give me ten minutes to shower."

I roll myself out of the comfortable fetal position I had myself in on the plush chair, dropping the blanket onto the floor. I stare up at him while I'm sprawled out, not wanting to make the final move to stand. Once I stand it's all over. I'll have to shower and leave my happy place.

He rolls his eyes before turning and walking back out the living room door, most likely to raid the fridge. He knows I made the long trip to Costco yesterday to stock up, so undoubtedly, he is filling up on anything he can get his hands on despite the fact that we are heading to a friggin' barbecue. That man is never full, how he stays in such great shape astounds me because he is always eating.

I'll never forget his momma complaining when he was a teenager about how much food her youngest son went through each week. Though he might be the youngest of the Thorne boys, he's the biggest by far. He outgrew his older brother by several inches. He reached six-foot-three by the time he was sixteen.

Twenty minutes later I'm dressed in my favorite pair of overall shorts and a red, orange, and green striped top while sitting in the passenger seat of his truck headed toward Jack's house. Jack is probably the guy he's closest to at the station; they both went through training together and have been good friends since. I like him, but there will inevitably be a lot of others there too, and some of them I'm not as fond of.

While I'm excited for all the food, the human interaction is something I could do without. Small groups and hanging out with good food or coffee I can handle. But out in the open with people I don't know who are chugging beers faster than they can eat their hot dogs? I have to pass.

"What are the rules today? How long do I have to stay in order to convince you to watch Outlander with me tonight? Nan is in Raleigh this weekend visiting her friend, plus she refuses to watch it with me, anyway. You know how I have to watch book adaptation movies and shows."

"Why is she refusing?" he asks, glancing at me from the driver's seat.

"Too much of a commitment. Her social calendar doesn't leave enough time."

"You want us to watch historical romance?" He glances over at me, a confused look on his face, before turning back to focus on driving.

"Well, yes. I want to see how the show compares now that I finally finished reading the whole series. Don't make me be the sad book girl who watches it all by her lonesome." A blush spreads across my face.

I know how sexy the books are, but I want to watch it and it's more fun to have someone to talk to about it when watching a show. If Nan won't watch it with me, then Griffin will just have to deal with all the sexy times. Hopefully, I don't die of embarrassment.

With a chuckle and a shake of his head, I know he won't deny me. For a rough and tough guy, he's pretty easy to convince to do what I want.

"You know, for a girl who I had to beg to leave the house, you're awfully needy."

"Only when it comes to you." I poke him in the arm, smiling, though doing my best to not let on just how needy for him I truly can be.

It doesn't take long to get to Jack's place. Griffin and he have been working together for years. Jack has always been the biggest flirt and serial dater up until he met Shelby. But in the span of the eighteen months, he met her, got married in Vegas, and had a kid.

It was a quick courtship.

Shelby works as an interior designer on the island. She fixes up huge houses for the rich people who will only use them for a couple of months a year. The cookout this weekend was her idea since starting Monday she's finally back at work since having their baby, Ava, two months ago. She doesn't really have any coworkers other than her assistant, Sarah, so Jack invited all the other firefighters and their families over too.

We park on the street along with a half dozen other trucks and a few minivans from the family men. He's out of the truck and over on my side before I can even get my things together.

"Hand it over," he demands, his palm up waiting for me to comply.

I play dumb, wide eyes and innocence on my face. "What are you talking about?" I climb down the too big truck, trying desperately not to fall over . . . again.

"The book that's hiding in your bag, Leni." He points to the tote bag hanging to my side. "Come on now, give it to me. Easiest way for you not to give in to the desire to hide and read is to remove the temptation."

"I left my book at home. Remember, you saw me set it down." I play dumb.

"I've known you since we were nine. If you think I don't know that you have a backup book in that bag, then you're dead wrong."

"Ugh!" I sigh dramatically as I pull out my well-loved copy of *Emma* and place it in his hand. He gently tosses it onto my seat, and I smack his shoulder as he does. He knows better than to throw around my books.

"Great, now the Kindle." His voice is stern, and I know he means it.

"Seriously? Griffin, this is not cool. I'm a grown woman. I can go a few hours without reading."

"Sure, you can. But I know you'll get overwhelmed by the chaos that is definitely happening in there and you'll retreat to a quiet corner." He leans in close enough to me that I can smell his subtle cologne and shoves his hand deep into the tote, pulling my Kindle out in one fast swipe.

"Don't you firefighters take obeying the law seriously?" I snark at him. "Seems to me you're stealing my possessions and my lifeline."

"Sue me. Hell, march downtown and file a report with any cop there. Good luck getting them to pursue it. I think they have much bigger fish to fry than me holding onto your electronics while we are at a social gathering. Don't you think?"

"Grrr," I growl at him before stomping off toward the gate with him on my heels. Before I can even acknowledge what is happening, he's caught up to me and has me caged between him and the gate. I work hard to steady my breath, refusing to let him see how his closeness affects me. I feel his hand slide into the back pocket of my overalls. As quick as it's there, it's gone, along with my cell phone. The backup to my backup plan.

"I told you, Leni, I know you. You can have this with your Kindle app back on the way home!" he yells out to me as I let the gate behind me slam in front of him.

With a huff, I turn, open the gate, and storm angrily through it. Caught in a fit of laughter, he stands there watching me leave him behind. With the loud sound of the metal gate slamming behind me mixed with the booming laughter coming from Griffin, the party seems to come to a complete standstill.

Great . . . everyone is looking my way and my first instinct is to turn and run. But to prove to him I can do this, I stand tall, throw my long red hair over my shoulder, and march myself over to Shelby.

"Welcome, Evangeline," Shelby greets me as soon as I walk through the gate to the backyard. "So glad you could make it."

"Thank you so much for letting me crash your cookout and congrats on the baby again." Besides books and my cat, baby cuddles are one of my favorite things in the world, so of course I stopped by the house after they brought little Ava home. But I still couldn't resist shopping a bit this week at the local baby boutique for another gift. I mean, is anything really more adorable than tiny clothes and mini stuffed animals?

"I brought you this." I pull out the small wrapped gift and hand it over to her. "I figured if you couldn't have it, then at least it can be added to the party pile." I hand her the bottle of wine I swiped from Nan's stash. I rarely ever drink, so I have no clue if it's any good. But based on the wide smile on her face she's either desperate for a glass after not having any for a while or it's a better bottle than I thought. Either way, she seems happy, so that makes me happy.

"Well, you are definitely always welcome here, hon." Her deep Southern drawl purrs the words out. Shelby moved to Scott's Bay two years ago to expand her buisness. I like to think we're pretty Southern here in North Carolina, but she is Deep South Southern.

I feel an arm wrap around my shoulders and instinctually lean into it assuming it's Griffin, but as soon as I do I realize my mistake. Instead of being much taller than I am, I can tell the person holding me is only a couple inches above my five-foot-three frame. The body is also much softer than my best friend's muscled firm frame. A pit forms deep in my stomach as I fear the worst.

I quickly turn my head to see the one person I knew it would be despite desperately hoping that I would be wrong. Ian Pharrell. He's a new firefighter, having started in the last six months or so.

Ian's the reason I stopped going by the station to visit and started asking Griffin to come to the library for lunch instead. I never told him about Ian's near-constant attempts to hit on me or pressure me to go out with him. I'd hate to create tension for him at his workplace.

Thankfully, he never asked why we changed meeting locations for our standing Tuesday and Thursday lunches. One of the best parts of my job is that the library is exactly three doors down from the fire station so even when he's on duty he's usually able to come by for thirty minutes to eat.

I try to wiggle out of his grasp without looking rude or drawing attention to what's happening. One raised eyebrow from Shelby lets me know the situation has not gone completely unnoticed. Great. Making it even more difficult to be nice and polite with my move is that Ian's fingers hold my shoulder tighter than necessary.

"Excuse me, I need to find Griffin. He has my phone and I gotta check on my . . ." Words fail me for a few seconds since I completely suck at lying. "My cat. He's not used to being left alone and my grandmother is gone. Anyway." I pull myself away from Ian before he has a chance to talk to me and ask me out for the twentieth time. "Thank you again, Shelby, for having me. Hopefully, we can catch up soon." I give Ian the evil eye and head out into the small crowd to look for my friend.

I finally find him in the kitchen holding a Corona while talking to Jack.

"I need my phone," I demand as I walk up to them with my palm out.

"I'm not watching that show tonight if you sit in a corner and read."

"I need to make a call," I tell him, pushing my hand, still palm up, closer to him.

He gives me a skeptical look. He knows Nan's gone and I don't call anyone but her and him.

"I need to call Toby."

"Really?" His words are questioning, but his tone tells me he's not even a bit surprised.

"Is Toby an ex?" Jack asks, clearly confused by our conversation.

"He's her cat," he tells him.

I adopted Toby last year when he kept wandering into the library. I couldn't just let him live on the streets, now, could I? I'm not sure how old he is, but if I had to guess somewhere around ten. He's a mean guy who only seems to like me and occasionally Griffin. He completely hates Nan. Not sure why, but they just keep their space.

"Okay, then." Jack steps back, his facial expression clearly showing how crazy he thinks I am. "I think it's time for baby Ava to eat, so I'll let y'all figure this out."

"Do I want to know why you need to call a cat?"

"I told someone I was going to. I needed to get out of a conversation."

"And you don't want to lie. Gotcha." He hands me the phone, knowing without explanation the importance of honesty to me. "But, Leni." He pauses and looks into my eyes with the sternest of glances. "I want it right back."

"Yes, sir," I say full of sass and I swear I see one side of his mouth tilt into a slight grin.

"We're really at this place in our friendship?"

"What?" I reply innocently.

"Don't what me," Griffin teases. "I know what happens in this show. I've heard all about it from Shelby. It's gonna get sexy, Leni. Real sexy." He winks at me, attempting to unnerve me. But I shall not be shaken.

I feel a blush creep across my cheeks. "It's just a show. Besides everyone has seen it by now except me."

"I haven't," he says, while he grabs some popcorn out of the microwave.

"Fine, fine. Just start the show." I plop down on the floral sofa. It's outdated and faded, but so comfy.

We've watched movies and shows together a million times. Hell, half of the time I end up asleep on his shoulder since I'm a notorious morning person and he's a definite night owl. In all those times we've never been so spread out.

The mood is definitely different as the show starts and already, I'm wondering if this was a bad idea. It's not like we haven't seen shows with sexy undertones before. But knowing this is gonna get graphic before we even start has us both acting a bit odd.

We're silent for the first few episodes. You can barely hear us breathing as the mood gets more intense. Yup. This was not my best idea.

"So, Leni, you've read the books? Were they masterpieces that are going to make your Librarian recommendation shelf next month?" The smirk on his face almost makes me laugh out loud. With the tenseness of the mood broken we're back to picking on one another.

"Stop teasing me!" I throw one of the million pillows on the couch over at his head.

"No, really, I'm curious. How were they?" His eyebrows are raised, but he's not laughing. His question is genuine.

"They were . . ." I struggle to find the right word. "Entertaining and well written."

He doesn't respond with humor like I would expect. Instead, he simply stands and runs his hand through his hair. "I'm gonna get some more popcorn. You want any?"

"Sure, grab me a beer too, would you?"

CHAPTER 2

Griffin
Nine years old

"H EY, BUD, GO OVER TO MS. HUGHES' HOUSE. HER granddaughter just moved in. She's nine too and doesn't know anyone here yet."

"Momma, do I have to really? The other boys are meeting down at the field. Mitchell got a brand-new soccer ball for his birthday and I really want to play with them."

"Now hush, boy. Go over there and invite Evangeline to go with you."

"No, Momma. I can't bring a girl. I'll get made fun of," I plead. "They'll say I like her."

"Don't be silly. You don't even know her. From what I hear from Helen, her momma's sick and I think it would be a good distraction if she had some friends. Now be the little gentleman I'm raising you to be and head over there and introduce yourself."

I kick the ground under me, knowing I can't get out of this, and nod. "Fine, ugh."

"Don't you ugh me, boy," Mom fusses at me. "Now take this plate of muffins next door and ask her to play."

I pout as I grab the plate from my mom and reluctantly head across the lawn.

"This better not take long," I whisper to myself before the front door is pulled open and a small girl with bright red hair and a face full of freckles answers the door. She might be my age, but she's several inches smaller than me.

"Sorry, did I open the door too slow?" she asks with her hands on her hips.

"Huh?"

"You said this better not take too long." She gives me a long glare. "Well, I'm not forcing you to stand on my front porch."

"Here." I shove the muffins at her. "I live next door. My momma made me bring these over here and told me to bring you to the park with me. My friends are all meeting there to play soccer."

"Thanks, and no, thanks." She's not even looking directly at me. Instead, she just keeps glancing over at someone in the living room just out of my eyesight.

Seriously, this girl's annoying. She starts to close the door and just as I'm about to turn to leave I hear a woman softly call out from the living room. I can't see her from where I'm standing in the doorway, but I'm guessing she's lying on the couch.

"Evangeline Marie, you cannot spend all day in this house," the faint voice tells her.

"I can too, Momma. I got a stack of new books at the library with Nan yesterday. I'm good for at least a week."

"No, baby, you need to get outside sometimes. And you definitely need some friends."

I stick my tongue out and then snicker at her getting handed her tush by her mom. I slowly start backing up down the few steps. She looks like she's about to take a swing at my head and I'm in no mood to tell my momma I got in a fist fight with the annoying girl next door. I'm just about to make a run for it when someone comes up from behind her.

"Git, you two," Ms. Helen, the girl's grandma and my favorite old lady on the street, yells from the hallway. "Peaches, let your mom have a nap. She'll rest better thinking you're making friends and adjusting."

The tiny girl's shoulders lower and what moments ago was a fighting mood softens with the mention of her mom needing the rest and comfort.

"Yes, ma'am," she says calmly to her grandma before turning back to me. The door that's been half-closed since she tried to send me on my way widens all the way back open. "Wait here." Her voice that was soft and calm just seconds before returns to its previous annoyed state as she says, "I'm getting my book first."

This girl is crazy. Great, I'm stuck with an insane tiny ginger-haired girl and I doubt this will be the last time. There goes my super awesome summer plans.

"I'm Griffin," I mutter, attempting to make small talk.

"I know."

"Okaaayyy, then," I draw out. "Was that your momma? She said your name was Evagasomething or another, right?"

She freezes mid-step to turn toward me. "Evangeline. It's not that difficult."

Sheeze, this girl.

"Okay, then, Leni," I reply, intentionally shortening her 'not that difficult' name.

After ten minutes of her silently walking behind me to the field, we arrive to the confused looks of Jefferson, Mitchell, Darrell, and Lucas.

Before I can even introduce her to the guys, she's taken off to a tree on the other side of the park, making herself comfortable with her book.

"Ignore her. Momma made me bring her," I tell the guys, pointing my thumb over my shoulder toward the crasher.

Two hours later, I'm sweaty and hungry, ready to head home. I grab my ball, the one I brought as a spare in case something happened to Mitchell's new one, and start on the walk up the dirt road back to the house. I get halfway there and realize I left something, or better yet, someone, behind.

Her.

"Well, come on, now!" I yell toward the tree she's still sitting under. "Catch up or are you just going to follow me slowly the whole way home?"

Slowly closing her book and standing, she brushes the grass and pine straw off her skirt before walking at a snail's pace toward where I'm standing.

"Hey, now, this was your idea. I didn't ask to be your friend. Remember, you came to my nan's house." I sure hope she and her mom aren't staying long. Momma said they moved in with Ms. Helen, but maybe she's wrong. Maybe she's just here for beach season and then will head back out in a few weeks. It's not like she's come around here much before visiting her grandma. They can't be that close.

"Momma made me," I spit back at her. I don't need this little girl thinking I'm happy having her tail me around.

"I don't like you," she says over her shoulder as she storms past me like she knows the way back. I walk a bit faster, determined to get back in front. No way do I plan on following her home.

"Good! 'Cause I don't like you either," I say with a smirk on my face as I pass her before running ahead and turning to the shortcut through the woods. Hah, maybe a long walk home alone will show her.

Three months she's been next door, my whole friggin' summer wasted. Felt like everywhere I went she was there. And of course, Momma constantly wants to stop to talk to her grandmother or mom. I can't escape the pest. She's got them convinced she's sweet and innocent, but I know every time they turn their backs, she's sticking her tongue out or rolling her eyes at me.

Today is Dad's day off and I wake too early, excited for all we are going to do. Dad is a firefighter and spends a lot of time at the station, sometimes whole days in a row. I don't get to spend as much time as I would like. He's often there before I even wake up for the day. But his days off are amazing. He spends the whole day with my brother Shane and me.

We grab breakfast at our favorite spot. We've been coming to The Breakfast Joint for as long as I can remember. The chocolate chip pancakes are the best I've ever had. By late morning we're stuffed and heading over to Surfside Beach. It's the best local spot since it's at the farthest end of the island. There's never a lot of tourists. No big hotels packed full of wild adults and their kids crowding the beach. It's my favorite way to spend the day and I take a moment to look out over the beach and ocean and of course, she's there under an umbrella reading a book.

"Ugh, seriously!" I yell out loud, walking off the wooden ramp down onto the sand as my dad stops to talk to Helen ahead of me. Shane is already down by the water's edge, and I'm just left behind by myself. What a great start to the day.

He looks up from his conversation to give me the side-eye. I know it was rude to yell, but I can't escape this girl. Everywhere I go she's there. Today was supposed to be the best day. Just me, Dad, and Shane throwing the ball around and attempting to bodyboard. But all day, I'll be watched by Miss Priss.

Hearing my yell, Evangeline sets her book down and turns around in her seat. The pure snarl on her face shows me she's not too excited to see me here either. As quickly as the snarl appeared on her face it was gone and immediately replaced with her pretend perfect child smile that has all the adults fooled.

Why can't they all see what I see, that she's no good? I'm always the one in trouble just because I'm a bit louder than her, but it's her who's always calling me names under her breath and sticking her tongue out when no one is looking.

"Well, hello, Griff-in." She drawls out the end of my name. "Figures you'd follow us to our spot."

"Shut up, Evagel-ine," I whisper back so I don't get caught telling her to shut up. "We've been coming to this spot forever. It's not yours. It's ours."

"Sure it is." Her words are agreeing with me, but the way she says them is the complete opposite. "Anyway, my nan's been bringing my mom here since she was a baby. Who do you think told your parents about it?"

"Whatever, it's more mine than yours. No one even bothered to bring you here until now. I've been coming for nine years."

Her face falls for a second, but before I can question if I went too far, her hard demeanor is back and she throws her long, wavy, ginger hair over her freckled shoulder and marches back to her chair. Can't say I'm not happy for the conversation to end anyway. All she does is suck the fun out of a good day.

An hour later and I've tried to ignore her, though I can feel her eyes boring into the back of my skull. A phone rings from her general area and I turn to see her grandma answer. I don't think anything of it and go back to throwing a frisbee with my dad.

After just a couple passes, I see Ms. Hughes walk over to where my dad is standing and start to talk to him. This can't be good. I sprint over to them just in time to hear the end of their conversation.

"Sure, Helen," he tells her. "She can stay with us while you take her in. Don't worry about it at all. She can even come out to dinner with us after the beach time. Ann would love it. I know she gets tired of only having boys around."

No, no, no. She has not weaseled her way into my day. I won't stand for it.

"But, Dad," I start to whine, but he isn't having it. I can't even get out any more words before his hand is in the air, giving the universal symbol for shut up. Not wanting to get in bigger trouble, I wait for them to finish talking. Once Evangeline heads back toward where her towel is and sits back down with her book, I prepare for the riot act I know I'm about to get.

"Griffin Cole Thorne, you do not act like that. That was rude and

I'm very disappointed. I know you and Evangeline don't always get along, but this is too much." His stern look and deep frown show me just how upset he is.

"I'm sorry, Dad, but this is boys' day. She can't just crash. It's not fair." I try to stand still in that moment while he talks to me like he taught me, but I can't help but kick the sand from under my feet in frustration.

"Not that I have to explain anything to you, but she isn't crashing. Her momma ain't feeling too well and Helen wants to take her to get checked out. She thought it would be better for Evangeline if she didn't have to go to the hospital with them."

"But why do we have to watch her? Can't she go be with Momma or somebody else that isn't us? This is boys' day."

"Your momma is out running errands right now and she's already here. Now stop being so selfish before you get yourself grounded."

I swear I will hate this girl until my dying day. She does nothing but ruin everything.

CHAPTER 3

Leni

T HE SUN IS PEEKING THROUGH MY SHEER WHITE LACE
curtains and I roll over until I've formed a blanket burrito out
of my plush down comforter. The air in the house is set to
frigid and even though it's probably eighty degrees outside it feels like
we're in the Arctic Circle in here. The joys of living with your seventy-
five-year-old grandmother who has zero fucks.

It's been almost a week since the cookout with Griffin, and it's finally my day off again. I have only seen him a few times in the past week
since he was staying at the station for most of it. After an hour curled up
in bed with the latest Amie Knight novel, I finally decide it's time to get
up and face the day. If I don't force myself away from my book early on,
then nothing will get accomplished all day.

Once I'm showered and dressed in my favorite sunflower yellow
sundress complete with a tan cardigan since it gets breezy this time of
year, I head out to the kitchen to fix breakfast for Nan and me. Back
when I was younger, Nan was up with the birds, but a few years ago
she said, 'Fuck it, I'm too old for alarm clocks.' Now she wakes when the
mood strikes, typically around ten in the morning, or on days like today
she rises when she smells breakfast on the stove.

I head into the kitchen and I'm shocked to see her already awake,
dressed, and actually sitting at the table with the paper.

"Hey! You up already?" I ask as I walk over to the stove, ecstatic to see breakfast is already made.

"Yeah, Peaches. Thought I'd make us some biscuits and grits. Been a while." She stands from the table and goes to stir the grits cooking on the stove.

"Mom's favorite. Thanks, Nan."

"Grab us some bowls, I got some gossip to tell you." Ahh, now I know why she's awake. The woman loves some good gossip.

Nan is everything I'm not. A social bee who loves to be in the thick of it with her friends. If I didn't know these ladies personally, I'd swear they were in their teens, not seventies. It's like living with one of the Golden Girls, only even more devious. I swear all of them go out looking for trouble.

Thankfully even though we couldn't be more different, we have always seemed to just get each other. Living through Mom's illness and passing, we really just had each other. Well, I also had Griffin, but no one else understood how it felt like Nan.

We both take a seat on the small white wooden table in front of the bay window. I close my eyes to take in the smell of the lavender I picked from the small garden Nan has growing in the backyard. Fresh flowers make the home. That's what Mom always told me when we were little and constantly changing houses. It didn't matter where we were, she always had flowers in a vase on the table. I enjoy the moment of peace before I open my eyes and see the excitement all over Nan's face.

"Okay, okay! Tell me! What's going on?"

"You know how yesterday the girls and I took a day trip across the bridge to the beach?" Nan pauses to take a sip of her hot tea.

We live in Scott's Bay, North Carolina. We are what the tourists call 'beach adjacent.' A curved tall bridge separates us from those with enough money to see the water every morning. But I'm not complaining. I wake to the smell of salt in the air and sound of the gulls flying nearby. For me, it's perfection.

"Yeah, y'all've been going every Tuesday for years. Beer at the beach followed by dinner and wine with dinner at Captain's Steakhouse."

"Well, we were making our way over the bridge when I see a familiar truck flashing his lights at me in the mirror. Of course, I can't just pull over. For heaven's sake, we are on a bridge! So, we just keep going with the pace of traffic and dammit he just did not give up. He followed us over the whole damn bridge. Well, I pull into the next parking lot ready to hear the riot act . . . again. Seriously, the girls on the cart were cackling the whole time."

"Oh, no, Nan, say it isn't so. Tell me I'm not going to start this day off with another lecture about road safety and how I need to get through to you. Please tell me y'all didn't do what I think you did." Pushing my plate to the side, I lay my head on the table in disbelief. Not that I should be surprised. She's been doing stuff like this my whole life.

"What? Since when is it illegal to drive a golf cart? We drive it all over this town."

"Nan, Griffin has told you a million times you can't take a golf cart onto the main highway and definitely not over the bridge. It's over half a mile long. You're lucky it was just him and not an actual cop. Why, Nan, just please tell me why?"

With a shrug of her shoulders and a small shake of her head, she indicates that she's gonna do what she's gonna do. Seriously, it's like the ladies in this town hit seventy and decide they have their own rules and laws.

"I swear, Nan, you stress me out. Isn't it me who's supposed to be the young one acting wild and reckless?"

"Well, you act like a grandma, so I figure at least one of us should be out there having fun and being a little careless."

"I'm fun," I say, hoping to convince her and possibly myself that it's the truth.

"Really, Evangeline? When was the last time you even went on a date?"

I start to shuffle my spoon around in my teacup, avoiding eye contact with the one woman who knows everything about me. She's very aware it's been over a year but honestly, I'm tired of wasting my time on guys who are just going to decide I'm too boring or quirky to put up with.

"That's not fair." I'm pouting and I know it, but it's a low blow. She's always been brutally honest with me. Especially with everything we went through with Mom's passing. But when it's aimed at me it's still a hard pill to swallow.

"Oh, Peaches. I know, but I hate seeing you just hang around here with me when you could be out in the world living your life."

"I live life. Plus, I live a thousand lives in the books I read."

"No, hon, I know the saying but none of those are the one you've been given. We aren't guaranteed our time on this earth. I just don't want you to have any regrets." She pauses for a bit as she looks out the window at the house next door. The one belonging to Griffin, the best man I've ever known.

"Don't even think about it, Nan." She's been pushing me for years to try for more with him. But that chance isn't worth the risk of losing him. Having him in my life means everything and I can't ever think about it being anything but what it is. "We aren't meant to be like that. I've told you that before."

"You have to risk a little to gain a lot, honey."

"He's not a little anything. He's all of me and I can't imagine ever not having him around."

"What happens when he meets someone else and starts a family?"

I gulp down the knot that's formed in my throat. "I'll be happy for him and I fully intend on being Auntie Leni." For someone who refuses to lie to other people, when it comes to Griffin Thorne, I've become an expert at lying to myself.

"You deserve more than that. Stop cutting yourself short." With that she gets up from the table we'd both previously sat down at and heads to the sink to wash her coffee mug before heading back toward her room to get ready for the day.

I'm still sitting at the table with my tea and Kindle when she emerges thirty minutes later dressed in some orange leggings and a sequined Halloween sweatshirt. She's got a shirt for every holiday.

"I almost forgot Halloween was coming up," I announce after noticing her attire. "I'll have to pull mine out of the back of the closet."

A few years ago, Nan started giving me some of her sweatshirts. I'm not one hundred percent sure if it was a joke or if she was legit thinking they were stylish, but either way I sorta look forward to wearing them along with her. It's odd, but it does make the little kids smile at our Kids' Corner time at the library.

It's after four by the time I leave the house and wander across the small lawn to the side door of Griffin's place. He's due to get off shift in an hour, and we have some serious TV night plans. I've been dying to watch more of *Outlander*, but he made me promise to wait for him. Seriously not cool. It's been a long week.

We rotate where we watch TV and movies, and even though it's my turn I figured having it over here was for the best. I wasn't prepared to get between him and Nan as he discusses road safety with her, again. He is the biggest rule follower I know, a Boy Scout to the core, and I think she likes to act out around him just to rile him up. I know the two of them are mostly just jesting around, but I can't help but get stressed.

Using my key, I open the side door that leads into the old kitchen. I step in and place the basket in my hand on top of the old worn-down kitchen table just to the left of the door before turning back and making sure to lock the deadbolt.

We live in the safest of towns, but still I'll hear it from Griffin if I don't lock up while I'm in here alone. I spend the next thirty minutes preparing the salad and putting the chicken pan pie I prepared earlier in the day into the oven. Ever since his parents moved to Florida a few years back and sold him their home he's been eating fast food and grilled cheeses unless we eat together. Once or twice a week when I'm cooking for me and Nan, I double the recipe and fill up his fridge and freezer. I just feel better knowing that he's eating good hearty food when I'm not with him.

Just as the timer dings indicating the food is ready, I hear the front door open. I walk over to say hey to Griffin and, turning the corner, I notice the harsh look on his face and the glistening sweat on his brow. Something is off.

"Umm, are you okay? I thought I'd surprise you with Mom's chicken pan pie for dinner." Chicken pan pie is one of his favorites, similar to chicken pot pie but no vegetables in it and instead of a crust it has biscuits on top. It's delicious.

A small smile crosses his face and the worry in his eyes is replaced with the normal twinkling I'm used to. Griffin Thorne is the nicest, sweetest man I know and if he wasn't my best friend, he'd be the sort of man I'd want to have a family with. He's going to make a woman happy one day. The thought of him moving on and another woman being the one to see him every day ties my stomach in knots, but having him in my life at all is better than asking him for more and risking losing him completely.

"No, this is great. I just had a long few days at work. I'm exhausted and I need a fun night with you after a really long week at the station. I had to work with Ian all week and if I have to hear him brag about all the girls he bangs when they are in town for vacation, I think I might lose my mind."

I bite my tongue from telling him all the times that scumbag has hit on me. As he puts his boots away, I can see him start to relax. Once he's got his stuff unloaded, he walks over to me and places a gentle kiss on my forehead.

"You're the best," he whispers as I instinctively lay my head on his shoulder, instantly feeling a comfort I've been lacking all week.

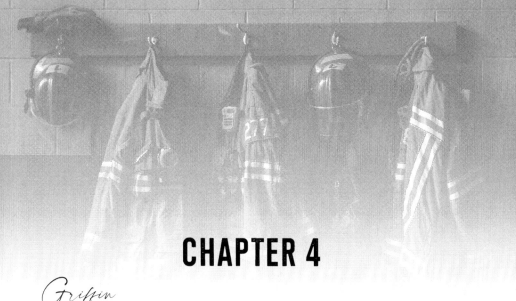

CHAPTER 4

Griffin
Thirteen Years Old

"WILL YOU HURRY UP?" I SHOUT THROUGH THE doorway to Leni, who's rummaging through a bag full of books she got yesterday at the library. "The bus is going to be here any minute, and Dad will have my hide if I have to ask him for a ride to school again."

"Got it!" She pulls a large hardback book from the bottom of the bag and holds it triumphantly in the air.

"Come on, Leni. The bus is here. We got to run. Hurry!" I hold the door open as she dashes past me, yelling bye to her grandmother on the way.

We barely make it and we're both forced to sit up front with the kindergartners so we can endure yet another lecture from the bus driver, Mr. Peters, on making the bus wait on us. He tells us yet again that we are supposed to be at the stop at seven twenty-five, ten minutes before the scheduled arrival time. Not running to the bus as it's pulling away, making us late to the rest of the stops on the route.

I nod in agreement all while giving Leni the death glare. She knows how much I hate getting in trouble.

"Sorry," she whispers, truthfully looking a bit ashamed.

Three months ago her momma died. We've spent the past

three-plus years hating one another, playing pranks, and overall trying to get the other in trouble. She was my enemy. Then the unthinkable happened, and I remembered how lonely and sad I was when my dad was hurt in a huge house fire before she moved to town. He almost died and it was the worst time of my life.

He's been a firefighter in our small quiet town my whole life. It's the safest place to live most of the year. Until summer comes around and the tourists fill all the empty houses and hotels. People are careless and reckless and every year it seems some sort of tragedy happens.

It was just two years before Leni came to live here, when he got hurt. He was in the hospital for almost two months. We thought he wouldn't survive. But I'm lucky. He lived and fully recovered. But I was terrified he wouldn't make it. I can't imagine how bad it is when you actually lose a parent.

Leni's mom had been sick since they moved in. It was just a fact that she'd been in bed or in her recliner chair. I honestly just expected her to stay that way forever and be there while Leni grew up.

But last year was when she got worse. Momma and I started visiting more, bringing dinner and trying to help Nan out. Before long, Momma was inviting Leni over to our house to hang out. She tried saying no and that she'd rather stay home and read her book while sitting on the couch near her momma.

But once she saw how happy it made her momma to see her doing things normal kids without sick parents did she stopped fighting it. I dreaded the days she would come over. She always acted like she'd rather read a silly book than play hide and seek or play tetherball in the backyard.

Occasionally she gets a burst of energy and runs past me yelling "Tag, you're it!" as she slaps me across the shoulder before taking off. But mostly, she hangs out in the kitchen with Momma or lying in my hammock reading some book that was way beyond our grade-level reading.

She couldn't be a more boring friend. But then her momma died. I didn't see her for a week. She stayed home with Ms. Helen and missed school. Momma took them meals, but I didn't know what to say or do, so I just stayed home.

When she came back, I started sitting with her on the bus. I don't know why I did it, but I did. She didn't complain and I didn't say anything. A week later I offered her my snack and the next day she asked if I wanted to come over and watch a movie after school.

I don't know how it happened, but in the last three months, she's slowly become my friend. It wasn't what I expected. A few months ago I would've thought this would be the worst thing to happen. But I like her, and I think she likes to hang out with me too.

"You mad?" she whispers to me, at least pretending to be apologetic. Even though she's softened since losing her mom, she's still retained most of her snark.

"It's fine. Hey, I have an idea. How about after school we go to the arcade? The one at the pier?"

"But it's always so busy." She slumps down in the seat, looking defeated.

"You are not allergic to people, Leni," I remind her as I put my arm around her shoulder. "You just like to pretend you are."

"No, I think they're allergic to me." Her head lies on my shoulder as the bus makes the short drive to school. I do my best to not look affected by her touch.

"Haha, come on. We've watched all the movies your nan owns. Let's please go out." I'm begging, but I need to get out of the house.

"You know you don't have to hang out with me every day? It's okay if you're tired of me. I know I'm not a ton of fun."

"Blah blah blah," I say with a smile. "You know I'm having fun. Plus, y'all got the best movie collection and your nan's stash of sweets is the best."

"Fine. We can go to the arcade, but we have to stop at the library on the way home."

"Really?" I say with a sigh. "Last time we were there for over an hour."

"I promise it'll be quick. I have a book I'm dying to read on hold. I just have to go in and grab it."

The bus stops in front of our small school. Living in a coastal town means there aren't a ton of kids here year-round. I've had the same kids in my class every year since kindergarten.

"Griffin!" my friend Micah yells at me as he climbs off his bus behind ours. "We're all gonna meet up to kick the ball at the park later. You in?"

"Naw, Leni and I are heading to the arcade after school. Y'all should come."

I feel her eyes burning through my skull behind me. She's not warmed up to the guys yet, and honestly, I don't think they've warmed up to her either. But my momma's right, she needs a friend who understands.

"Yeah, maybe. We're gonna go shoot some hoops," Mitchell says in our direction while pointing to the guys behind him. "Maybe we'll come by after."

"Sure," I reply a bit disappointed. I know they won't show. "Sounds like a plan."

Hearing his reply is all Leni needs to grab the hem of my T-shirt and start pulling me toward our street.

The walk home from the arcade is long and we have to cross the huge bridge. Momma had to go to work at the diner and Dad was still on shift, so we headed back over the giant curved bridge. Thankfully, it has a walking section with a fence between the road part and us, but I can tell it freaks Leni out. We've only walked it one other time these past few months and she kept a death grip on my hand the whole time.

Our local library is unfortunately only two streets over from where we live. This means I've spent more time there since starting to hang out with Leni than I have my entire childhood in Scott's Bay. Every time we go, I browse the outdated kids' sports illustrated magazines while she picks out more books than she can hold. Books I know I'll be helping her carry on the way back home.

"Leni, please hurry. I'm starving." I'm peering at her through the books from one aisle over. Every time she moves down, I move too and push the books aside so she can see me.

"Shhh," she whispers loudly at me from the next aisle over. It's an old building with small rooms, but in each room, they've crammed as many shelves full of books as they possibly could.

"Seriously, Leni," I snap back. "There is no one here but us and old Ms. Sanderson. Plus, she's deaf and passed out behind the desk. She couldn't hear us if we were playing tag in here."

"It's a rule. I thought you never broke rules."

"You need to live a little." That gives me a genius idea. Before she can respond I run over to her aisle and tap her on her shoulder from behind. "Tag, you're it."

"Absolutely not!" I barely have a chance to see the shocked look on her face before I'm off and running.

"Catch me and I'll read any book in here you want. Promise," I call out from over my shoulder.

"You? Willingly reading a book, not for school?" She feigns a fake, shocked face while holding back laughter. "You know we could get in trouble, right? Wasn't it you who gave me lectures on honesty and following rules when we met?"

"Seriously, Leni, I was a ch-il-d." I play it off, even though I really don't want to get caught. I hate letting my parents down and I practically get hives just from thinking about lying to anyone.

"Griffin, you're only thirteen. You know that, right? You're still a child," she tells me before sticking her tongue out playfully.

"Hmmh, I'm basically full-grown. But you are avoiding the topic. Find and catch me before Ms. Sanderson wakes, and I will read any book you choose. Don't and you have to let me teach you to play soccer."

She freezes and I can tell she's actually thinking over my offer. Before she can talk herself out of it, I tag her arm again and run off.

I find the perfect hiding spot and tuck my small body into the tight space as best I can and attempt to slow my breathing. I'm determined to win this. No way will I be spending my weekend with a book. Not when the sun is out, and the air is finally cooling off. This is the perfect weekend for kicking the ball around.

I hear the sound of her tiny feet passing by and attempt to be as silent as possible. If I can just stay here long enough for her to give up, then I will win.

"Griffin, you little turdscicle. I will find you and I will hurt you." She's giving herself the most ridiculous pep talk and a small chuckle escapes my mouth and immediately I know I've given away my location.

Before I have the chance to steady myself in the twisted-up position that I had to force my body into in order to fit into the small already pretty full cabinet, the door is yanked open and I tumble out onto the floor.

"Aha!" she yells at the top of her lungs before slapping her hand over her mouth at the realization of just how loud she truly is being.

I don't hesitate. Years of playing with some of the most devious boys around have taught me to act fast and waste no opportunity. I jump to a stance before she has the chance to tag me and take off in a full-on sprint down the aisles.

I hear her giggles hot on my tail and I can't help but join in her laughter. She's chasing after me full speed ahead. Quickly I turn the corner and run smack-dab into the large soft stomach of Ms. Sanderson.

"Mr. Thorne," she says firmly, hands on her rounded hips. "There is no running in the library."

Leni clearly didn't notice my swift stop because just as the words escape Ms. Sanderson's mouth, Leni runs directly into my back and falls backward on her bottom.

"Miss Hughes!" the sourpuss librarian gasps out loud. "I expect this behavior from rowdy boys, but you, my dear, I thought understood the rules of the library more than anyone else. You basically live in here."

I expect to see tears forming in Leni's eyes when I turn back to her, but I'm shocked to see her jumping to her feet, her hands firmly on her hips as she imitates the librarian's position.

"Ms. Sanderson, that's not fair. Griffin is a good kid, there is no reason to expect him to be rowdy just because he is a boy and I'm a girl. If anything, he is a better rule follower than me, typically. I do not appreciate your lumping us based on gender. If you are going to accuse him of being rowdier than me based on personal experience, then that is fine, but it's not because he's a boy. If anything, it's because he's a turd."

I hold in my laughter at her snarky response.

"Now, I apologize for our behavior," she continues, finally relaxing her shoulders.

"I do too," I add. "I'm sorry. I was just trying to help Leni have a little fun. Show her there is more than books." Based on the glare she's giving me I'm guessing my excuse isn't exactly helping my case. Goodness, I should just keep my mouth shut.

"Hmmh," the cranky old lady replies and I hold back my eye roll. "I think maybe y'all should leave for today."

"Yes, ma'am," we respond in unison, not wanting to get in any more trouble than we already were. We are just about to walk out when Leni has a realization. She pauses and turns back to face the librarian.

"Could I check my book out, though?" Leni asks, a worried look on her face as if not getting her book today would be the worst possible outcome. "And Griffin here wants to check one out as well."

"I do not," I inform the old woman.

"Yes, you do. I found you." She sticks her tongue out and waves the book she picked out for me through the air.

"I do not," I tell the old woman, ignoring my annoying friend, before I turn to Leni. "And you did not tag me."

"I did too." She stomps one foot on the floor, letting her temper show.

"You did not." My voice escalates.

"Children!" Ms. Sanderson bellows, startling both of us. "I think you should leave. You may return tomorrow if you need to check anything out. We open at ten in the morning."

"Please, Ms. Sanderson, I have nothing else to read," Leni pleads, even though we all know she has a million books.

"Fine," the old lady reluctantly agrees. "But make it quick."

We're both silent for the first few minutes of the walk home. I know Leni is pissed, but I also know she had fun . . . until we got caught.

"I'm sorry, Leni," I start but before I can continue, she's already talking.

"Listen here, Griffin, I found you and you owe me one book. That's fair."

"You did not catch me. That was part of it. I say you owe me one soccer lesson."

"How about a compromise?" she suggests. "How about tomorrow morning we go to the field and you can show me how to kick a ball? But afterward, we sit under the tree and I read a book out loud while we eat some sandwiches."

"Fine. But at least make it an exciting book. Nothing long and boring."

"Fine, but first we are going to the library and you better not get me in trouble again."

"Deal," I reluctantly agree as we resume the walk back to our street. With the new book in her bag there's a skip in her step. She's a bit ahead of me and I need to catch up, but I allow myself to take another minute or two longer trailing behind her.

Lately I can't help myself from staring at her. She's caught me a couple times and I had to play it off as if she had something on her face. At this point she's probably convinced she's the world's messiest eater.

I'd rather her think that than the truth, which is that when I look at her mouth all I can think about is if she'd let me kiss her. I can't have a crush on my best friend. I just can't. Other kids in our small class have started pairing up and many already assume we are a couple because we're always together. But not Leni, she's oblivious to it all.

After looking at her skipping in front of me for a few too many minutes, I run up behind her and tap her on the shoulder as I yell out,

"Tag! You're it!" Before I take off down our street and hightail it to my backyard and up into my tree house.

"That was not fair, Griffin Thorne!" a panting Leni yells from the bottom of the ladder up to where she knows I'm hiding. "You don't have anything but a soccer ball in your backpack and you know mine is full of books." Dropping her bookbag on the ground, she starts climbing the ladder up all the while giving me the glare she perfected back in our enemy days. I know she isn't really mad, but that doesn't mean it's still not a bit scary.

"That's what you get for carrying all those books around. Can't be light on your feet."

"You'll rue the day you insulted my books!" she yells out. "Rue!" She bursts into laughter before we both fall down onto the bean bags in the corners of the small tree house.

"Leni?" I hesitantly ask.

"Yeah," she responds while digging under her bean bag for the book I know she's stored there. "What's up?"

"I was wondering. Are you going to the seventh-grade dance next Friday?" I ask as I look over her head. I know if I make eye contact it will give away everything I'm thinking.

"Nan says I have to. Something about not being anti-social." She's already flipping through the pages of her book to find where she left off.

"Oh, yeah? I was thinking I might go too." I want to go with you. With you with you. I want to say. But I don't. Not yet at least.

"Duh," she says, already nose deep into a book I know she's read a million times.

"What do you mean duh?"

"You like people, Griffin," she tells me with a shoulder shrug.

"I don't like everyone." I lean against the side of the tree house, staring down at her.

"Who don't you like?" She actually puts the book down to look up at me as she asks this. As if the idea of me not liking someone is so absurd, she needs eye contact while I explain.

"I didn't like you for a long time, remember?"

"Yeah, but now you love me."

If she only knew.

"You want to go with me?" I ask in one breath, scared out of my mind.

"Duh," she says again as if it's no big deal. "You're my best friend. Who else would I go with? Plus, Nan already told your parents she'd drive us. I'm gonna need you to help me hide a book in the gym earlier that day. She already told me I can't bring one."

Okay, we're going, but as friends. I'll take it. For now.

CHAPTER 5

Griffin

"**I** GOT BURGERS. WHO'S HUNGRY?" I ANNOUNCE AS I WALK into the mostly empty library that Leni recently took over as head librarian. It's been her dream since we were kids.

"Hush," she whisper yells to me, making me smile.

"Chill, Leni, there isn't a car in the parking lot. I think it's safe to talk at a normal volume." I walk over to the checkout desk where she is leaning on her elbows looking over a stack of papers, a scowl I know too well covering her face.

"It's the rule, don't act like you don't know." She tucks the strand of red hair that has fallen out of the mess sitting atop her head behind her small ear as she grabs the greasy brown bag out of my hand and pulls her favorite burger out of the white Cook Out bag. Typically, she's a fairly healthy eater, but I know her weakness.

"Rules are meant to be broken, Leni," I reply, teasing since she knows I rarely break rules unless they are arbitrary ones like whispering in an empty library. "Otherwise what's the fun in life." If only she really knew how many rules I wish I could break with her. Sometimes I worry my deviant mind will take over and I'll accidentally say something I can't take back.

"Hush. Give me a minute and if everything's good we can go sit in the break room."

When Linda, the other librarian, arrives and settles at the desk, she leads me toward the break room in the back of the small library. It's an old historic train station the town turned into a library forty years ago. Having grown up here my whole life, not to mention lunch here once or twice a week, I know my way around. Still, I don't stop her when she grabs my wrist and pulls me through the large front room to the old kitchen in the back that now serves as a break room for the two employees and the couple of high school volunteers.

"What's the hurry?" Her pace is more rushed than usual, and my interest is piqued.

"Linda said she saw two police cars outside old man Perkins' place. I've never wished harm on another human being in my life, but that man is a grump. Tell me someone at least TP'd his house."

I can't help but spit the small sip of tea I just drank from the cup that's been in my hand since I arrived. Only Leni would, as a grown woman, think toilet papering a man's house was the worst thing she could think of. She's a spitfire but also the nicest human I've ever met.

I'm surprised she cares at all about Leonard Perkins. Hell, last year he led a campaign to try and convince everyone that running the historic library was a waste of town resources. Of course, no one voted for that, but still, it irked the hell out of Leni.

I've never seen her hold a grudge against anyone else, but he was her first.

"Don't get too excited. He called in a complaint against his neighbor next door to him because she let her dogs out to pee too many times and he claims they are a nuisance." One of the perks of being a firefighter in town is that we hear all the police calls too. If something happens around here, we're the first to know.

"Doesn't she have a fence?" she questions before drinking some of her sweet tea.

"Yup," I mumble out, my mouth full of burger.

"Hmm," she says under her breath as she takes a giant bite of her burger.

"I know that look. Whatever you are thinking you better put a pause button on it. You don't want to end up on his bad side. You know that he's a vengeful old man. Has been since his wife Betty died."

"I'm just gonna take him some cookies. I'm making some anyway for the new neighbor across the street. She moved in not long ago and I haven't made any time to go introduce myself," she explains before taking a huge bite out of my burger.

"Stay away from him. I'm telling you this screams of bad idea." I stop eating to look at her. I know I can go a bit overboard sometimes, but I'm just trying to protect her.

"That man has to have a soft spot somewhere. We can't just go on having him terrorizing this town." She tries her best to convince me she'll be fine.

"He ain't terrorizing no one, he's just a pest with too much time."

"That's your opinion, Griffin. Mine is that he's a grump who needs to learn the difference between right and wrong."

This woman has been driving me insane for too many years and today is just another day of it. For someone who hates to leave her house she can't help but get involved when she deems a cause "worthy" and apparently setting Mr. Perkins straight is worth the trouble.

Before I know it, lunch is over and I gotta head back over to the station. Luckily, we're in the off-season and it's pretty quiet around here. A few more hours and I actually get a couple days off. I'm exhausted and ready to sleep for forty-eight hours straight.

Not fifteen minutes after I arrive back the alarm goes off. I rush to get in my gear, and we head out across town.

"What are we looking at, Captain?" I call out to the station captain, Greg, who's sitting up front.

"Hopefully just another false alarm, but we got a call about a small fire over at the new Chinese restaurant in town."

It doesn't take but three minutes for us to arrive at what is definitely not a false alarm. Smoke is coming from the open front door. We get our ass in gear and luckily put it out before the grease fire spreads to the front of the restaurant. Thank goodness someone called it in right away instead of assuming they could have put it out themselves. It could have been so much worse.

I'm finally off shift and I'm exhausted. My bed is calling me. I drive myself home, ready to change into some sweats, eat whatever I can find that fast, and pass out. Today's shift went way over. By the time we put the fire out, made sure everyone was okay, got back and filled out the paperwork and got our gear put away, it was a good hour past the time I was supposed to leave.

As soon as I'm in the door I see something sitting on the counter. A huge smile crosses my face as I walk over to it to see a note taped to the top that says 'You work too hard to have just a bologna sandwich. Eat some stew and get some rest. See you tomorrow. Leni.'

I swear if it wasn't for her, I'd be eating fast food most days. I grab the note off the top of the Tupperware and flip it over to draw a little picture of a cartoon Leni sleeping and a little cartoon me eating, and I write a thank you on the top. I throw the food in the microwave before picking the note up and walk back through my living room to the front door.

My feet are killing me, but I slip my boots back on and walk across my lawn to the little red box outside her window and drop it inside and lift the little bar on the side up, like you would on a mailbox. Thinking about her getting the doodle in the morning brings a smile to my face as I make my way back to my place.

I've always been into drawing but just as a hobby and I started leaving her ones taped to her window when we were ten or so. By the time we were in eighth grade, I'd fashioned the mailboxes out of some scrap wood I found and, in the years since, it's been our own little way of communicating.

Back in our teen years on the occasion that we had a fight we always made a point to still answer the mail we would leave in the boxes outside our windows. Even if we were pissed and only responded with one word we'd always write back. As we've aged we don't use them as often as we used to but still some days I'll come home and see the bar on the side of my box pointed up and I feel a bit of a rush as I check it to see what she left me.

My schedule has been insane recently since I've picked up some overtime to help me earn a little extra money. There are some projects on the house I'd like to complete when I take my time off next month and I'm not about to put that on a credit card. Unfortunately, that means I haven't seen Leni as much as we're used to and tomorrow, I finally have a day off and we have big plans. As soon as I'm back inside I scarf down the food she left and immediately pass out in bed, ready for the next day.

My eyes crack open and the sun is bright through the window. I could've sworn I closed the curtains last night.

"Seriously, you should probably wear pajamas to bed or at least some sweats. What if some stranger broke in and found you looking like that?" the curtain opening culprit says from the end of my bed. I jump, not realizing she was here.

"Only person sneaking in here is you. Learned your lesson the hard way." I quickly pull on some pants while I hear her giggling as she heads out of my room. Rarely is she up before me, so I didn't think I'd have to worry about her coming in my room this morning.

"What time is it?" I mumble, making my way toward the smell of fresh coffee.

"It's beach time," she says with way more energy than anyone should have this time of day.

"Are you feeling okay? You're actually wanting to go out in public?"

"The beach during October isn't public, no one is there. Plus, I have a real good feeling about today."

Every year since we were younger and started to hang out together willingly, we've gone to the beach during the off-season to see who can find the most intact and perfect shell. When we were kids it was just a way for our parents to get our energy out so we would go to bed, but we've kept it up over the years. Nowadays, we've made a competition out of it and whoever gets the best shell has to buy the other lunch at

Captain's Steakhouse. Our favorite seafood restaurant and one of the few that actually stays open year-round.

"All right all right, but let me grab a quick shower, and then we can head out."

"You better be bringing your wallet because I have a good feeling about today." I've just finished my shower and barely have my jeans on when I see her in my bedroom doorway.

She's silent for a good two seconds as I dry off my scraggly hair before she grabs the shirt I have sitting on the bed and throws it at me. A couple of minutes later, I head back out to the kitchen to find Leni in her apron standing at the stove.

"I made some egg sandwiches for our breakfast. We can eat on the way, but I packed light because you are definitely treating me to some crab legs tonight."

"You're awfully cocky. You didn't by chance do any reconnaissance, did you?" My Leni never lies, so I know if I ask if she's trying to be sneaky, she'll tell me.

A piece of bacon hits me in the chest and I quickly grab it up. "I can't believe you would accuse me of cheating."

"That's not an answer."

A second piece hits me.

"No!" she says, wrapping the sandwiches in paper towels. "But Nan did tell me she saw some good ones on her walk yesterday. But I wouldn't let her give me details nor did I grab the map she tried to give me this morning. Plus, I've won like the last five times. I'm on a roll."

"How is it that woman hasn't gone to jail yet?"

"Pretty sure she's too clever to get caught."

"Hmmh," I grumble. "I live in fear every day of when I will inevitably hear of her arrest and know I'll end up being the one bailing her out. The boys at the station will never stop ripping on me."

Twenty minutes later we pull my truck up to the public parking lot and grab a spot right next to the ramp to the beach.

Leni jumps out, giddy as a child.

"Isn't this weather the best?" she proclaims as a gust of wind coming off the freezing cold-water hits me in the face. She's always loved the beach during the off-season.

"Sure, if you're a bit of a psychopath. But I'll let it slide because you are too adorable in that getup."

"Are you making fun of me?" She places one hand on her hip and the other she uses to adjust her sweater, which currently features Snoopy dressed up as a ghost and a giant pumpkin carved to look like Woodstock.

"I wouldn't dare. I love your seasonal sweaters. I know no one is gonna kidnap you in that outfit."

"You got jokes." She jabs her elbow in my side as she lets out a giggle and the most beautiful smile. This is the Leni I love. The one others don't get the joy of seeing. She's hilarious and flirty and loves to give me hell. Other people see her as the quiet girl with her nose always deep in a book. But for me she becomes this whole other person. One I want in my life every day however she'll let me have her. I don't think I could ever tire of her.

We walk in comfortable silence side by side as we both look at the ground for treasure. Thirty minutes pass before anyone says a word and that's the amazing thing about Leni and me. It's not even a little bit awkward. We can be talking all night or just together and quiet. It doesn't matter when we are together.

After four hours of walking and talking on the beach, we finally head back to the truck. I'm exhausted and starving, but it was a great day.

"I can't believe you won," she says, climbing in the passenger seat. "You never win."

"Not true! I won three months ago."

"I let you win."

"You did not! I won fair and square," I respond like a scorned five-year-old having a fight in kindergarten.

"You were pouting on and on about work and your lack of a social life. And since the town has, according to you, decided you are undatable for some reason, I took pity on you and threw the amazing perfect conch into the ocean so you wouldn't see it."

"Sure. If you say so," I say, knowing she's telling the truth since she never tells a lie. It's at times a very frustrating quality to have in a best friend. "But today, I won fair and square, so dinner is on you! Ha!" Yeah, apparently, I'm still in kindergarten. But whatever, free food is free food.

"I know the rules. Now take me to Captain's! I'm hungry for some crab. Momma wants to eat good tonight."

"Did you just call yourself momma?"

"Shh. Just go with it. My hunger might be driving me slightly crazy."

Laughing, I put the truck in drive and take us to our favorite joint.

CHAPTER 6

Leni

I CAN'T SLEEP IN TODAY. I'VE TRIED, BUT I JUST KEEP WAKING UP.
Usually, I can stay up reading all night, then if I don't have to go to
work, I'll sleep past breakfast. But not today.

That's why I'm sitting on the front screened-in porch with a giant
mug full of coffee. Yummy, sweet, delicious coffee. It's my vice. I drink
it all day full of sugar and creamer. Preferably the yummy creamer that
comes in flavors like Almond Joy and Sugar Cookie but in a pinch regu-
lar coffee with a ton of milk and sugar will do. It's probably why I'm up
some nights until two in the morning reading.

But, oh well. What's a girl who lives for coffee and books to do?

Looking out onto the quiet neighborhood always makes me happy.
I love our little street. We all know each other, which isn't surprising because, if you don't count tourists, this is a very small town. Most coastal
cities around here are. That's why I noticed the new people across the
street last week. I keep meaning to go over and introduce myself and
take a little something to them, but I've been too busy. But today is my
day off and the day I finally do it.

I knew the house had been up for rent since the owners, Ben and
Julia, decided to move to Asheville where their kids and grandkids now
live, but I hadn't seen anyone there. Just as I'm wondering who might be
there, I see Griffin come outside in his work clothes. Something about

the fireman uniform just makes any man look like he's straight out of a romance novel.

"Hey, Griffin," I call out as I step down off the porch and cross my tiny yard over to his.

"Morning. You working today?" He looks at my faded floral night-gown up and down.

"Got the day off," I tell him. "But, I got a quick question before you head out?"

"Shoot," he says, while leaning into the truck to set the travel mug of coffee into the drink holder.

"Do you know who moved in across the street?" I point my head in the general direction of the small house that had up until recently been sitting vacant.

"Seriously, Leni?" He blinks in apparent astonishment at my question.

"What?" I pretend to not know where he's going with this.

"You sit out there every morning reading and you have no clue who moved in over there?"

"We can't all be super observant like you are," I fight back.

"I love ya, but sometimes you amaze me how in your head you can be."

"Well . . . who moved in?" I ignore his statement, determined to get the gossip.

"I've seen a man and a woman, so far. But I've been working a lot, so I don't know much more."

"Maybe I'll go over and say hi later, be neighborly." No clue what came over me, this is not something I would typically do. But knowing your neighbors is normal and I need to work on expanding my horizons.

"Look at you peopling. I'm proud," he jokes.

"Ha ha, I told you I'd try, and this is me trying."

"Well, good job, I gotta get to the station, but I'll be back later. Just a day shift today."

"See you then. Be safe." I say that every time he leaves for work.

I'm still mad he went into such a high-risk job, but I know it's been his plan since he was two. He's the spitting image of Dale, his dad, from his incredibly good looks to his kind soul. There was never any doubt he'd end up a fireman just like him.

I knock on the door of our new neighbor across the street as I balance a plate filled with my famous lemon cookies. They just moved in last weekend and with everything going on I haven't done the neighborly thing and taken something I baked over and introduced myself.

Several minutes pass and I hear someone rumbling around inside. I decide to knock once more. If no one answers I guess I'll just take the treats back over to Griffin's. I'm just about to give up when the door cracks open and I see a girl who can't be more than eight staring back up at me.

"Hey, sweetie, is your mom home?" I ask in my calmest librarian voice.

"Nope, but if you find her let her know I've been looking for her for two years."

Well, okay then. Not sure how to respond to that.

"Oh, okay, how about your dad?"

"Well, seeing as how he ran off a few days ago with some woman I think was actually named Princess I don't expect to see him for a while."

Is this a child? Or some strange non-aging adult? I'm used to kids being silly, but this girl is all stern and talks as if she's already fully grown.

Just as I start weighing the need to call Griffin to look into getting child protective services out here, a young woman with a raggedy robe on and a towel wrapped around her head comes flying around the corner.

"Sorry, sorry," she says toward my general direction before turning her attention toward the little girl still holding the door open. "Mikaela, what did I tell you about opening the door to strangers?"

"Make sure I only open for handsome ones without wedding rings on?"

The woman's shocked expression tells me that was not what the child was told.

"No one. You open the door for no one," she corrects her.

"Hi," I interrupt, not knowing what else to do. "I'm Leni, I live across the street." I point to the general direction of my house and Griffin's place. "I noticed y'all moved in recently and thought I'd drop by to introduce myself, and of course, bring by some cookies."

The two of them just stare at me before the little girl, Mikaela, nudges the bigger one in the side.

She jumps to attention and reaches out to grab the plate. "Thank you so much. This is too kind. I'm Parker and this is my niece, Mikaela. Ignore whatever comes out of her mouth. Before me, she was raised by rabid wolves."

"This is true," Mikaela interrupts. "What kind of cookies are those?"

"They are my famous lemon cookies with sprinkles on top."

"Oh, hmm. I guess I'll try them, but chocolate chip would have been better."

"Noted," I respond. I'm used to the bluntness of some children, so I don't give her the shocked response she's clearly expecting. She grabs a cookie from the top of the pile and heads over to the couch on the other side of the room to watch what sounds like basketball on the television.

"Sorry, come on in." She opens the door wide and I step through despite my hesitation. "Would you like some coffee? I'm just gonna throw some clothes on real quick then I'll join you."

"That would be great. I'll just set these in the kitchen." I make my way through the living room to the small but adorable kitchen. The place is set up just like Nan's house, so I know just where to go.

I set the plate down on the small painted wood table in the corner. It's purposely distressed and super adorable. Everything in here is country chic and looks to be handmade or at least updated. I'm giving myself a tour of the adorable decor when I hear Parker come into the room.

"I love all the distressed furniture and cute items. Your place is adorable."

"Awe, thanks. Updating and repurposing old and outdated items is a hobby of mine. I haven't had much time for it lately, but I do love it."

I'm still looking around the room while she starts a pot of coffee. By the time it's done, she has mugs out on the table and we both sit and relax. The next half hour passes in a flurry of small talk. She has a million questions about the town, the schools, and just life in general. It's clear she doesn't have many friends to talk to.

By the time I head out the door I've learned that she just started waiting tables over at the small diner in town and it was just recently that she got custody of her niece, though I didn't get any backstory as to why and I didn't want to pry.

I don't have a ton of girlfriends, but she seems sweet and fun and we already have a coffee date at the library planned for later in the week. This might be the first time in a long time I've been excited to hang out with someone new. I want to show her some of the resources we have on hand that can probably help her as well as introduce her to Griffin if he swings by around lunchtime.

My day off went by in a blur. Between baking all morning and spending time with Parker across the street, it's almost dinner time and I haven't even had a chance to swing by Mr. Perkins' place to bring him some cookies in hopes of making him even a smidge less of a turd.

The front door swings open with force and in walks Nan, arms loaded full of plants that will inevitably die. About twice a year she gets convinced she can have houseplants and within weeks they all start to wilt.

"Here, let me help you," I tell her as I make my way over to where she's struggling.

"Thanks, Peaches." She's just about to drop one when I get there.

I take half the plants and set them on the kitchen table.

"Any particular reason you've sentenced these lovely plants to die?" I shake my head, thinking she'll never learn.

"Hush, child. This time I promise to not overwater them. The nice man at the nursery showed me this lovely app that will tell me when it's time to water each one. He even helped me put all of them into the app and set today as the first day to water," she explains, though even she doesn't seem convinced it'll help.

"If you say so. I'll believe it when I see it," I jokingly tell her. "Hey, I'm going over to Mr. Perkins' place to drop off some cookies. You wanna come with me?"

"Why on earth are you going over there? That man has a stick shoved so far up his ass you can see it in this throat if he opens his mouth." Her hands are on her hips and the sour puss face she's making says it all. She's not a fan.

"Lovely image. But I think he can be brought over to the good side. If we show him some kindness, then maybe he'll show someone else some." I give her a small hug and her ill demeanor vanishes and is replaced by my sweet, yet insane, grandmother.

"Pretty sure that man is a lost cause but have at it. I'm exhausted and he's a pill. I think I might have to pass."

I grab my small brown crossbody bag and the plate of cookies I have covered in Saran wrap and head toward the door. "Yeah, I get it. I shouldn't be long."

Five minutes later I'm pulling into Mr. Perkins' driveway. His lawn is well manicured and every two feet along the top of it by the sidewalk are small yellow signs saying, "Pick up after your dog."

This man isn't playing. I leave the car on while I run up to the porch, not wanting to get caught up staying long. I'm starving for dinner and I honestly don't really want to go inside. I knock three times on the door but even though I can hear someone moving around inside no one answers the door.

I walk back over to my car and grab a pen and paper out of the glovebox and write a quick little note telling him the cookies are for him and I hope he enjoys them. Setting them on the small table on the front porch, I yell inside, "I hope you have a good day. I brought you some cookies."

I don't know if I'm let down or relieved that he didn't answer, but either way I feel good about doing a nice thing.

CHAPTER 7

Griffin

"WHEN YOU GONNA MAKE A MOVE, BOY?" HELEN'S voice comes out of nowhere as I sit behind the driver's seat of my truck parked in the library parking lot waiting for Leni to get off work. I came by earlier and noticed her car was way past due for a check-up, so I drove it over to the mechanics and had them give me a ride back to the station.

"Dammit, Nan, I've told you not to sneak up on me like that."

"Aren't you supposed to have the reflexes of a ninja or something like that in your line of work?"

I shake my head at her remark. She's the only one who can get up on me without noticing. She's like a superhuman grandma. I stopped questioning her abilities years ago.

"So when you gonna tell her?" She nods toward the building where Leni is currently finishing closing up.

"Don't know what you're talking about," I say, playing dumb, working hard to steady my face to not give away how much exactly I understand. How desperate I am to do what she's saying.

"Do you think I'm stupid, child?" She leans into my window for a second, invading my personal space, something she has never really cared about.

"You know I don't," I tell her as I drop my head in preparation for the lecture that I can tell is coming. One I've swindled out of hearing from her for far too long. I've become an expert of sneaking away whenever she hints at me and Leni being more than just friends.

But she's got me trapped in my truck and I can't leave without Leni, I promised her I'd be here and I'm not gonna let her down even though I know she could probably catch a ride with her grandmother. On second note I bet that old biddy would refuse to give her a ride just because she knows that if she doesn't agree I won't leave.

"I've watched you tiptoe around this subject since you first turned into a horny teenage boy. You might think you're good at hiding how you feel, and to her, maybe you are. But anyone who's been in the same room as the two of you knows how you feel."

"Have you been drinking?" I ask curtly.

"Just a couple beers at lunch and a glass of wine during happy hour. But that's not the point." She's leaning against the truck next to the window and I can't tell if it's to help keep her upright or if it's just a better position to lecture me from.

"What are you even doing here? I don't see your car. I swear you just apparate in places."

"I was shopping at the boutique across the street and saw you sitting here."

I glance over across the road at the only store there. I've lived here my whole life. I know every place in this town but still, I can't help but confirm that she was actually shopping where I think she was.

"You were over at the Tease 'Em Lingerie Boutique?" I ask and immediately regret the words as my ears take them in.

"I'm old, not dead. Got myself a hot date tonight. Not all of us plan on going to the grave sad and alone."

"That's not the plan," I whisper under my breath.

"Yeah, well, then you better act on how you've been feeling all these years. It's about time you stepped up to the plate. She loves you, but you know as well as I do that she's scared of getting close and losing anyone. And you are the person who would hurt her the most in the world to lose. Not me, not anyone else. You. She's never gonna make the first move. Hell, she probably isn't going to make the tenth move. But she loves you. I see it every day."

With that, she turns and walks back across the street, not even bothering to say goodbye. Five minutes later, the library door opens and with a big smile on her face, Leni locks the large old red wooden door and walks across the parking lot to the side of my truck. She's a vision in a pink and white sundress with her red hair piled high on top of her head in a messy bun and her favorite pair of large black-framed glasses sitting high on her nose.

If anyone else had this getup on I would think they looked like an old lady, but on her, it's sexy as hell.

"Good day?" I ask as she climbs into the truck.

"It was. As you know, story time days are my favorites. Plus, Parker from across the street from us and her niece Mikaela stopped by and I talked Mikaela into trying out the Babysitter Club books. They were my favorite at her age. She was hesitant but after a while of me telling her why I loved them so much she left with the first one. I can't wait to hear what she thinks."

I won't break her heart and tell her the girl probably only agreed so she'd stop talking about them. I remember how relentless Leni was as a kid trying to get me to read. I can't even imagine her determination now. Maybe she really will read them, but I won't hold my breath. I head out of the small parking lot and drive toward the car shop, not sure if I should bring up the whole Nan buying lingerie and dating thing.

Deciding I can't keep it a secret from her, I try to branch into it carefully. "So how's Nan doing lately?"

"Oh, you know Nan, busy as a bee."

"Yeah, she's been hanging with the girls?" I question, pulling into the shop lot. "Or has she made some new friends? Maybe some of the male variety?"

She turns her head to look over at me and stares at me for a good thirty seconds before replying.

"Why would you ask such a specific question? What do you know, Griffin Thorne?"

"Ran into Nan earlier while she was shopping, and she was coming from the shop across the street and she happened to mention something about a hot date tonight," I blurt out in one breath before quickly opening the truck door and walking across the lot to the shop's lobby.

She sits in the truck silently for a few seconds as she realizes what shop I'm talking about because suddenly she is no longer quiet at all. The door to her side of the truck is thrown open and she's out and following behind me with quickness.

"Ew, ew, ew," she calls out as she follows hot on my heels. "Nan. Lingerie. Hot date!" she says a bit too loud just as I open the door to the shop. Everyone inside turns to look our way before going back to what they were doing before.

"Yup. That's all I know, but I had basically the same response when she told me."

"But why didn't she tell me?"

"I don't know. Maybe it's new and she doesn't want to upset you? Or maybe she thought she did one night after drinking with the girls. I wish I knew." I ring the bell for service and thankfully Leni drops it, though I'm sure it's not the end of it.

Once we get to her car, we each head back to our side of town in our own rides and though I get stuck at a yellow light miss daredevil decides to cruise on through. She's already inside her house probably grilling Nan when I pull up to my place.

Just as I'm getting out of the truck, I see her book on the floorboard of the passenger side. My head drops because I'm exhausted and desperately want a hot shower, but I know full and well I'm gonna take the book over there because it's the right thing to do.

I grab it out of the passenger side and head across their small lawn and through the screened-in porch to knock on the door. Not something I typically do, but it feels right knowing they might be having a serious conversation.

Nan yanks the door open with a force and gives me the death glare before declaring, "Remember, boy, snitches get stitches." As soon as it's out of her mouth she's stepped back and walked out of the room.

With a deep breath, I enter the house and quickly find Leni sitting at the dining room table.

"Seriously, how fast did you drive to get here and question her? When we left you were only one light ahead of me."

"I needed to know. You know I don't like secrets." Her hands are firmly on her hips; she means business. But no matter how hard she tries, my Leni could never look intimidating. She's just too pure for that.

"I know, but damn." I run my hand through my dirty-blond hair, which is very much in need of a trim. "What did she say?"

"Only that he's an older man that she met last week when she was out with the girls and that they are going out for a nice dinner tonight."

"And the lingerie?" I cringe at myself for asking. The regret hits immediately.

"She just said that matching bra and panties put her in a good mood, which I know is true for most girls, myself included."

I casually pull at the collar of my uniform T-shirt, hoping she won't notice. The thought of her matching bra and panties has me quickly becoming harder than I'd like standing here in her and her grandmother's living room.

"You staying for dinner?" she asks, standing up from the table and heading into the kitchen.

"Sure sounds good. I'm just gonna run over to my place real quick to clean up and change into some more comfortable clothes. I didn't get a shower at the station today and I've been sweating in my uniform all damn day." I place a gentle kiss on her forehead. "I'll be back in just a couple minutes."

I jog over to my place and unlock the door before taking the quickest shower, allowing myself just enough time to work out the thoughts of what she's wearing under that sweet dress today.

Twenty minutes later, I'm back over at her place and helping to chop some vegetables for tonight's dinner. We've done this enough times that we already know how to work as a team and don't even really need to communicate to each other what to do.

Nan emerges just in time for the food to be ready, somehow avoiding all the prep work and cooking. Clever old lady.

"Smells good. I'm starving," she says, sitting down at the table, helping herself to a heaping helping of chicken stir fry and rice.

"Thanks," we both respond at the same time.

"Don't you have a hot date?" Leni asks her, voice filled with sarcasm.

"Not until nine. We're meeting for drinks," Helen responds smiling. "Maybe more."

We all eat in casual conversation; just as we have several nights a week since Leni returned from college a couple of years ago. The two years she was gone finishing her degree were the worst and I was terrified she'd end up moving away permanently. Every single day she was gone I missed her. We constantly talked and visited, but it's not the same.

I lived in fear that that would become our permanent reality. There aren't a ton of positions for a librarian around here. But she was determined and worked there part-time until she was able to take over.

Being here with them is as comfortable as being back at my place. Maybe even more so since Leni is here and I'm happiest when I'm near her.

"You can really thank us by washing up after." Leni follows up with.

"Sure, babe. Y'all relax." We both stare at Helen in disbelief before looking at each other and quickly making work of putting our dishes in the sink before she changes her mind.

"Great. I'm getting some tea. You want a beer?"

"That'd be great." Leni's never been a drinker. I think the idea of letting loose and giving up control is too far out of her comfort zone. But sweet tea, that she drinks by the gallon.

"It's a nice night. Let's chill outside. Go on out, I'll meet you there in a minute."

I sit myself down in the old Adirondack chair, praying not to get a splinter. These things are so old I once got a two-inch piece of wood through the leg of my sweats. They need to be replaced, but like everything else in their place unless it's broken and beyond repair, it's there to stay.

Leni walks out with a tall glass in one hand and a bottle of my favorite beer in the other. Toby is right on her heels ready to curl up in one of our laps as soon as we're settled.

CHAPTER 8

Leni
Seventeen Years Old

"CAN YOU TELL ME WHY PROM IS A THING?" I YELL OVER TO Nan as I try on the third dress out of the twenty or so she picked out for me.

"It's a rite of passage, child."

"Ugh, but why am I going again?"

"You said yes to Patrick and it's your senior year. Now, let me see the next dress on you."

When he asked me last week I completely froze. Boys have never really shown interest in me. Though according to Griffin, they have, but my nose is always buried too deep in a book to notice.

When Patrick McIntyre cornered me last week before second period I had no clue what to say. Instead of telling him I was hoping to go with my best friend I just said 'sure.' Part of me was happy to be asked, but a bigger part was sad that it wasn't Griffin asking. Over the past few years I haven't really given dances a second thought, but if I did imagine going with someone it was always Griffin.

Now here I am in Wilmington with Nan trying on dresses and trying desperately to think of any way to get out of this. Prom is in one week and when Nan found out I had a date she immediately made hotel reservations for us to go to the "city" this weekend and get everything I needed. I tried to tell her I could just wear a dress I found in our town, but she insisted they would have all been picked over by the girls who made plans on going months ago.

"So, who is Griffin going with?"

"He asked Hallie the same day Patrick asked me. I'm surprised he waited that long, but I guess he was indecisive over who he wanted to take. You know all the girls got a thing for him."

"The same day," she repeats back. "You don't say."

"Yeah, well, I guess with it being a week away the guys who didn't have dates yet must have realized they were about out of time."

"Yup, sounds like they had a fire lit under them. What's Griffin and his date's plans? Are they getting a limo?"

"Naw, that's not really his style. We are gonna double date. Griffin talked to Patrick and they made reservations at Captain's."

"Your favorite restaurant!" she exclaims as I open the dressing room door and walk out in a dress that fits like it was made for me.

"Evangeline," she sighs, taking me in. She never uses my full name. Ever since Griffin donned me Leni that's what everyone has called me. "That's the one, it's perfect."

"You think?" I ask even though I have to agree with her. It's amazing. It has a soft blueish gray lining with delicate gold lace overlay. The sweetheart neckline lies perfectly, and the A-line skirt has a slit all the way up to my thigh. I couldn't have dreamed up a better dress.

"Now that one looks like a keeper," the saleslady says in a sing-song voice.

"Yes, we'll take it," Nan tells her as she wipes what appears to be a tear out of her eye.

"Leni, where are you?" I hear Griffin yell just as the door to my room bursts open. I quickly slam shut my journal. I don't need him to see all my mind-less doodles, no less than half of which are of his and my names together.

"Good job at knocking," I tease, tossing a stuffed bear that happened to be on my bed at him.

"Shouldn't you be full into prom prep mode by now?" He steps farther into the room until he's sitting on the edge of my bed. I will my heart to stop beating so fast. I'm not supposed to react this way. He's my best friend. I'm lucky to have him in my life at all.

"What's to prep? I put on a dress and shoes and we all meet outside."

"Only you could get away with just throwing something on and come off looking as great as the other girls who spend all day getting ready."

I refuse to think too much about his words. He's just being kind. His date is one of the prettiest girls in our school. No way I can compare, not that I'm trying or anything.

"Well, I just wanted to check on ya. Make sure you aren't backing out tonight." Lying back sideways on the end of my bed, he puts the bear I'd thrown at him just a few minutes ago behind his head as if it's a pillow.

"Couldn't if I wanted to. Nan spent all this money on the dress and the trip to the city. I couldn't do that to her." Opening the drawer of my side table, I put my journal safely away before, standing up to walk over to my closet to look at the dress hanging in there waiting for me to actually wear it.

"There's also the whole not standing up your date part too," he points out as he sits back up.

"Yeah, that too," I say without a ton of enthusiasm in my voice. "Wouldn't want to be rude."

"I gotta head back home and get showered and throw my tux on. I'll see you out front around five?"

"Yeah, we're all gonna meet then," I say just before he heads back out. I hear him yelling bye to Nan, then the screen door shuts.

Griffin arranged with Patrick for us to double date tonight. We're all gonna take his truck to dinner, then head over to the hotel for the dance. I'm just happy I don't have to go at this alone and will have Griffin with me even if he's really with another girl.

It takes me twenty minutes to get dressed and tame my wavy hair into submission. I didn't do anything fancy with it, opting to just put some frizz control product in it and pull half of it up into a ponytail.

Just as I hear a knock on the door, Nan comes out of her room.

"That should be Patrick," I say, making my way through the living room.

"The boy can wait a second, I have something for you." She stops me in my path to the front door.

"You've already done too much."

"Nonsense, child, but this isn't something I bought. Well, not for you at least. Sit down here." She points to the ottoman in front of the comfy green chair that sits adjacent to the couch. "This was the hairpiece your momma wore to her prom. I was going through my old jewelry box the other day and came across it."

She shows me the most beautiful delicate gold clip. It's a figure-eight made of intertwining vines. Walking behind me, she pins it into my hair onto the part that's pulled up.

"Now you're ready. Go answer the door before that boy starts to wonder if you're coming at all."

I freeze for just a minute staring into the mirror in the short front hall. It barely looks like me. Honestly, I look more like my mother than I ever have. Before she got sick she was always so stylish and put together. She loved all things girly and having this little piece of her with me makes me happier than I ever thought I would be tonight. I miss her every day, but at least for tonight it feels like she's here too.

I pull the door open and see my date standing there, a corsage in his hand and a nervous look on his face.

"Here, this is for you." He hands over a beautiful purple, almost blue, corsage.

"It's beautiful. It's a peony," I say, smiling down at it.

"Yeah, Griffin let me know it was your favorite flower."

Of course he did. Bastard is determined to make my night perfect. He ought to focus on making his own date's night perfect.

"Oh, I was supposed to get you one too, wasn't I?" I exclaim, realizing I messed up.

"Never fear, Nan is here!" I hear as Nan comes barreling into the room with a clear box holding a single rose corsage. "Picked this up while I was out earlier. Figured you might need it."

"Thanks," I say, feeling slightly ashamed that I forgot. I need to get myself together before it becomes glaringly obvious to him that my heart is not in this date.

We all three head outside where we are meeting Griffin, his date, Hallie, and his parents for pictures. After forty-five minutes and too many pictures to count, we all four pile in Griffin's truck and head over across the bridge to the island where Captain's is by the oceanfront.

The place is packed and I'm not surprised. Not only is it prom night for our small school but being May it's also the beginning of the tourist season. Thankfully we have reservations, so we don't have to wait long.

We're seated in my favorite spot, right by the window overlooking the water. I might have lived here since I was nine, but I'll never tire of looking out over the water.

"Miss, miss?" I must have gotten lost in thought looking at the seagulls eating fries that have been dropped on the deck outside the window because the waitress, whose name tag tells me her name is Sandy, is staring me down.

"I'm sorry, what?" I ask as the three other people at the table are all looking right at me.

"She'll have a large sweet tea. You might as well go ahead and bring her a pitcher. It'll save you a lot of effort. She's gonna need about fifteen refills," Griffin tells her. He knows me too well.

"Sorry, thanks," I tell him while Hallie gives me the evil eye. I guess she doesn't like her date ordering for me.

The whole table falls silent while we look at the menu.

"You getting the stuffed tilapia?" Griffin asks me and I already know what he wants.

"Yeah, you getting the shrimp and we go halfsies on both?" I ask since that's what we typically do whenever we go out to eat seafood.

"Duh," he says, closing his menu.

"But, babe," Hallie whines while twirling one of her blond ringlet curls around her finger. God, I can't stand her. "I thought maybe we could split a lobster and steak for two."

"Naw," he tells her, not even getting that she's upset. "The shrimp and tilapia are better here. They have a combo platter for one of the steak and lobster. If you really want it, I guess you could get that."

"I'm gonna get the scallops," Patrick pipes in, seemingly oblivious to the tension that is currently at the table.

Luckily, after we order the conversation quickly changes over to our senior projects and what each of us is doing. I'm almost finished with mine, but the other three still have lots to do. I eat mostly in silence, letting the three of them carry the weight of the conversation.

By the time we arrive at the hotel, prom is in full swing and Hallie grabs hold of Griffin's hand, pulling him out onto the dance floor. He follows behind her while turning his head to look at me. He mouths sorry before the two of them disappear into the crowd.

"You wanna dance?" Patrick asks as he puts his arm around my waist. I try not to shrink into myself, but it's too late. He notices and pulls away.

"Umm, sure." We head into the crowd just as the song changes from some pop tune to a slow song. I follow his lead and put my arms around his neck as his arms come around my waist. It doesn't feel right, but this is what we're supposed to be doing here. This is the whole point. But as good a guy as he is, he's really not who I want to be with. Still, I made a commitment and I will not be the person who bails.

I let him pull me in tighter and lay my head on his shoulder. Even if he's not Griffin it still feels good to be wanted and he's a good guy. I decide to stop being upset about my circumstance and just allow myself to enjoy the night.

Two songs later we break for some punch and see Hallie and Griffin over by the refreshments.

"Hey," I say, walking up behind them. "Having a good time?"

"The best," she answers for him. "He's such a great dancer. All the other volleyball girls want a turn with him, but I keep telling them, 'Sorry, ladies, he's all mine.'"

The sting of her words gets to me for a second, but I hold my shoulders high.

"Hey," Griffin whispers into my ear as his date gets distracted talking to one of the girls from the volleyball team. "Save me a dance, okay?"

I nod, unsure of what to say.

"You promise?" he asks, looking in my eyes.

"I wouldn't lie," I respond without hesitation.

"I know, but I still want to hear it."

"I promise, now you better get back to your date before she notices." I take a few deep breaths to calm my racing heart.

"Yeah." He looks down at his shoes. "You're right."

Two hours pass and I don't see him again other than a few glances here and there, but I don't even really notice because I'm having a good time with my date. He's surprisingly funny and smart. He's even read several of my favorite books.

Prom is almost over and I haven't seen Griffin again. I'm guessing he forgot about our dance. I try not to be disappointed, but I can't help it. I had a good night overall, but knowing he forgot about me hurts a bit. I miss him and was looking forward to having at least one special moment tonight with him for me to look back upon.

"I'm gonna hit up the ladies' room. I'll be right back," I tell Patrick because I don't want him to see the sadness on my face. After giving my face a quick splash of water and a little pep talk, I head out of the bathroom.

"You hiding out in there to get out of our dance?" a voice calls to me just as I walk out.

I quickly spin around to see Griffin leaning against the cement brick wall just outside the bathroom.

"Stalker much," I joke as I give him a little shove on his shoulder.

"You know it!" He gives me a wink before grabbing my hand. "You owe me one dance. Now, come on."

Letting him lead me, I walk just behind him, not even attempting to loosen the grip he has on my hand. If he's Hallie's for the night, then I'm gonna enjoy the next three minutes while I pretend he's all mine.

As soon as we're on the dance floor, I wrap my arms around his shoulders, not needing him to nudge me at all. His strong arms wrap around me and we're torso to torso. It's intense and intimate, at least for me.

"Did I tell you how beautiful you look tonight?" he whispers into my ear.

I shake my head, not sure I can talk right now. Instead, I just bury my head in his neck and listen to him whisper the sweetest words into my ear.

"You are stunning tonight. Just gorgeous, Leni. But then again you're always the prettiest girl in the room."

Usually I would give him a shove or tell him to stop teasing me, but for tonight I'm gonna allow myself to pretend that those words are real and the way he's holding me will be forever.

CHAPTER 9

Leni

IT'S MOMMA'S BIRTHDAY AND NAN AND I HAVE A TRADITION. One that started when I was just fourteen, the year after she passed. We were both still dealing with grief every day and Nan woke up on Momma's birthday and decided that even if we still were living in sadness the rest of the days that year we would put on a smile and celebrate the life Momma lived. Our tradition has evolved over the years, but the sentiment and the celebration have never changed.

"Rise and shine! The sun is up, and the day has started," Nan announces as she bursts into my room at eight.

I set my book down on the nightstand and slide up in the bed. "How are you already so cheerful?" I ask her, yawning.

"Probably because I didn't stay up until two in the morning reading." She pulls the curtains open, letting the day flow in. "Also, I treated myself to some Bailey's in my coffee this morning. Now get up, girl. We got a full day ahead."

"Need coffee. Must have coffee."

"It's on the kitchen table, girly. Get up, drink up, and let's hit the streets."

Exactly one hour later, I'm dressed, caffeinated, and ready for a day of fun and debauchery . . . with my grandmother.

"So, what's first?" I ask, looking over at Nan, who is sitting in the passenger seat as I back out of the driveway.

"First, we are getting breakfast."

"Yes!" I interrupt. That has been one part of our yearly tradition that hasn't changed since the first birthday after we lost Mom. "I've been looking forward to it all week. The grits, the hash browns, some fried eggs. Not to mention the delicious pancakes."

Nan lets out a small chuckle and I don't blame her. The Breakfast Joint is a longstanding spot here in Scott's Bay that is only open until two in the afternoon and they only serve breakfast food. This place has been a love of mine for too long.

When Momma was well enough, we'd go there together every Sunday morning and she'd let me get whatever I wanted. No kids' menu for this girl. Nope! She knew breakfast was my favorite meal and she wasn't gonna force me to only have one small pancake and some scrambled eggs.

She never got mad if I couldn't eat everything I ordered. She'd put on a big smile and declare that all it meant was that we got to have breakfast for dinner that night. She was awesome, my momma. But when her health started to decline things changed. Nan would offer to take me there, but it wasn't the same without Momma being able to go with us. For too long I just suffered through breakfasts at home or other sub-par places. That is until one day Momma apparently had enough of it.

Despite barely being able to sit upright in bed she found the strength to let me know I was not going to miss out on the best things in life. No, I was going to eat the food, do all the things, and live my life.

From then on, every Sunday morning Nan would run over there to get our food and bring it back and I would sit by Mom's bedside and eat while talking my week over with her. At first, I tried to eat in the kitchen, but she insisted I eat it in her room so she could smell the smells and pretend we were back here celebrating making it through another week together.

"What now?" I ask, wiping my mouth to rid my face of the mess I made devouring the best meal I've had in a long time. With a belly full of pancakes, grits, and sausage I'm as ready for whatever is coming as I'm gonna get. Nan loves to keep the day a surprise for me.

"First, we're gonna go say hi to your momma followed by some pampering and makeovers. I have it all booked."

"We don't need makeovers. There's nothing wrong with us."

"Of course there isn't. We're fabulous. But getting pampered and buying a new outfit is fun. Plus, while your overalls and white T-shirt are cute, it's not gonna work for what I have planned later tonight."

"Should I be scared?"

"Oh, baby girl. After all these years, don't you know you should always be a tad scared when I set up surprises? It's my life force. Getting you out of your comfort zone is what I live for."

"Greattttt . . ." I say as I sink down into the booth while we wait for the bill from breakfast to come.

Nan's wide smile and devious eyes are all I need to know that she's ecstatic about my reluctance.

"Fine," I relent. "Surprise me."

We head to our next stop, Momma's grave. I come here often, at least once a week to catch her up on life and just to keep feeling that connection to her. It's no longer a sad place but a place that brings me joy. I tell her things I couldn't tell anyone else and it feels so good to let it all out.

I stand back up and see Nan sitting in the car on her phone, probably gambling or swiping right on Tinder; could be anything with her. Seeing me heading toward her, she rolls the window down and leans halfway out.

"Come on, pretty girl. We got places to be."

Shaking my head in disbelief that not only are we blood-related, but other than Griffin she's the person I spend my time with.

I hop in the car, buckle up, and put the key in the ignition.

"Okay, where to?" I wait for the address to put into my GPS. But of course, she doesn't make it that easy.

"Head south on Emmett Road," she just says as if that makes any sense.

"I don't mind driving, but if you are gonna use words like south just be prepared to get royally lost."

"I can drive us. Just switch positions." She starts to unbuckle her seat belt and mine!

"Oh, no, missy, I'm not about to let you drive. Did you even get the parking tickets you have taken care of? Have you gotten your license back yet?" I roll my eyes and then snap my seat belt back into place.

"I'm working on it. But I'm fine. I can drive."

"Nope, not happening. Just put an address into the map app on my phone. It'll tell me how to get there."

"You know you would have died in the desert back in my day. No app that talks out loud telling you where to go." I desperately attempt to talk sense to her.

"Despite there being absolutely no deserts anywhere along the east coast, I'm perfectly aware I would not have survived. I've learned to live with the anguish of not being able to read a map or navigate based on the sun and stars."

I pass my phone to her and she reluctantly types in an address I don't recognize. I place the phone back in the holder and start the twenty-five-minute drive to the new "secret" location.

Twenty minutes later, I pull up in front of a fancy pants salon. I knew this was coming, but I figured we were going to Great Clips as usual. My salary does not allow me the luxury of going to expensive places with the word Salon in the name. Plus, I'm not really that sort of girl. I just can't justify giving up my days off at a spa or salon when I could be reading. But if Nan wants to go here, then I will go with the biggest smile on my face.

"Helen, long time no see," a blond woman calls out from the other side of the place as we walk through the double doors leading into the most ornate space I've ever seen.

Chandeliers hang from the ceiling, plush velvet walls, and those fancy mirrors the beauty bloggers have with the lightbulbs all around at each station. I feel overwhelmed as I look around, but then I look over at Nan, who's currently wearing zebra print leggings and a sweatshirt with sequined lips and lipsticks all over it. I'm still standing by the door and she's sashaying across the floor blowing air kisses to all the people waving to me. Apparently, my grandmother has a whole secret rich woman life I knew nothing about. I jerk back to reality and rush to catch up to her.

"Friends of yours?" I ask as we walk to a back room.

"You know Doris." She pauses then she looks up at me to make sure I'm following along. "Well, her daughter opened this place last year and her mom has been making her give us girls half off services since then."

"They all seem to like you." I shouldn't be surprised. It's impossible to not love Nan. She's a blast. Plus, she's thoughtful and always willing to get into a bit of trouble for the sake of her friends and a good time.

"What can I say? I'm a good tipper." With a wink and a smile, she turns away from me and enters the room we've been led to.

I immediately notice two massage tables in the center.

"Ladies, Maurice and Fiona will be with y'all soon. In the meantime, please undress as much as you're comfortable with. We've left robes and champagne just over there." She points to a glass and rose gold table.

"Thank you so much, Kathleen. Tell your momma I said hey and I can't wait for our pub crawl next week."

"Will do, and y'all enjoy." Kathleen clicks a remote and the lights dim, and the sound of ocean waves comes from speakers around the room. She then exits and shuts the door.

"I call the woman," I announce as I turn to find Nan already stripped down to her skivvies. "You don't waste no time, do you."

"Hush, no need in putting off the stripping. Can't get a good massage if you're fully dressed. And you sure about not taking the man? It's been a while since you've been touched by a man, hasn't it?"

"Too far. Too, too far." That woman has zero boundaries. "But yeah, I'm sure. I won't be able to relax."

"Fine by me, sweet cheeks." She downs a glass of champagne and hands me one as she grabs her second. When in Rome, I guess.

Two and a half hours later we've been rubbed, had our hair done, faces done up, and nails painted. We finish off our last glass of champagne and head out with Nan having already taken care of the bill.

I head out the front, car keys in my hand, when I notice Nan isn't beside me anymore. Nope. Instead, she's still on the sidewalk pointing to the boutique store next to the salon.

"Come on, Peaches. We're going in here. We need new digs for our night out!"

"Digs, Nan? Who are you? And what night out? There is a perfectly good book waiting at home."

"Oh, no, you don't. We're not wasting our spectacular looks on a book and a night alone. Nope. You and I are hitting the town."

Dropping my head in exhaustion, I head back across the parking lot and follow her inside the clothing store. Stepping in, I'm immediately hit with the smell of perfume and the sound of some current pop hit blasting so loud you could hear it over the halftime show of the Super Bowl.

"Nan, don't you think we're a bit too old for a store like this? This is more club age youth clothes."

"Youth clothes, Evangeline? You do know you're still in your twenties. I swear sometimes I think you're older than I am. You need to live it up a bit."

"If you say so." I follow her through the racks of barely there clothes and crop tops until we reach a section of what I can only describe as a place where sequins go to die.

Within two minutes, Nan is throwing several outfits into my hands and I'm being directed to the changing room.

"Umm . . . you do realize these clothes have an abundance of sequins and a deficit of fabric."

"Hush, child. Now try on the green one first. It's my favorite."

After hanging the other two up, I pull the green one off the hanger, determined to make Nan's day. That is until I get a good look at this so-called dress.

"I can't even wear a bra with this. Also, is this a shirt or a dress?"

"Oh, just put it on and get out here!" she yells at me. "Stop stalling."

After sliding on the dress, I stare into the dressing room mirror, not sure of who I see. This is definitely not me. But I have to admit, this dress fits me like a glove. I've never put anything like this on. Usually, I prefer my cute sundresses, rompers, and overalls. This is so far out of my comfort zone, it's not even in my comfort county.

Slowly, I open the door and exit the dressing room as if I'm in *She's All That*. Only instead of it being Freddie Prinze Jr. and a staircase built for a dramatic entrance, it's my grandmother and a store clerk desperate for some commission and I'm leaving a dressing room in a store I normally wouldn't step foot in.

"Oh, sweetheart. You look amazing," Nan says after taking my full makeover in. "You remind me so much of your mother right now. With her red hair, green was always her color too. We're getting you that dress and then we are heading over to one of Nan's favorite joints, Port Haven."

Port Haven's a bar over on the island side. It's where the tourists hang out in season and out of season. It's full of townies every night looking to get laid. It's not the sort of place you'd find a librarian and her grandmother, even if your grandmother is convinced she's still in her twenties. But where Nan is concerned, nothing is truly surprising.

"Why are we here?"

"You need to loosen up! And where better to strut your new look than at this hip bar."

Seriously, how is she my grandmother? If I didn't adore her so much I'd demand a DNA test. I know I'm not going to win today, so I hold my head high, straighten my shoulders, and make my way into the unknown.

"You win. But just one drink."

"We'll see! We will see!"

I push through the small crowd up to the bar where I spot two seats beckoning us. Just as I set my purse down on one, someone else grabs the other one.

"Oh, I was saving that one for—" I turn behind me to point out Nan, but of course she is nowhere to be found. There aren't a ton of people here, so if she was still at the bar I'm pretty sure I'd see her.

"For who?" the mystery man asks, looking around.

"My grandmother, but it seems like she's ditched me."

"How about I'll sit here and help you save it for her?"

"Sure, I guess." I'm still looking around for that sneaky woman. She's probably halfway home by now. This is entrapment. She's tricking me into dating. "Seems she's abandoned me for now."

"Well, then, you won't mind if I buy you a drink while we wait?" He waves the bartender over and orders us two drinks, a rum and Coke for him and an apple martini for me. Awfully presumptuous of him, but maybe he's trying to impress me.

The drinks come in no time and I quickly down mine. I'm not usually a drinker, but after the day I've had I think I might need one or two.

"That was tasty. Thanks." I go to stand to call Nan to come and get me. I had a drink with a man, even if I downed it in zero point two seconds.

"You don't have to rush off. I just ordered us one more round."

CHAPTER 10

Griffin

T HE DAY IS OVER, THANK GOODNESS. I'M EXHAUSTED AND ready to head to bed. I spent the majority of the day pulling old tile out of the hall bathroom and laying some new tile down. Not a huge change, but if I want to fix this place up, I gotta start somewhere.

I'm just turning on the hot water for the shower in my bathroom when I hear my cell start ringing. It's after nine at night and I haven't heard from Leni all day. I'm guessing she's calling to tell me about her and Nan's day. I turn the shower back off and go over to where the phone is sitting on the bedside table. A quick glance at the caller ID shows me it's not her at all. It's actually Nan.

"Hey, everything all right?" I already assume something must be wrong. Nan doesn't call me often, but when she does, it's never a good thing. Usually to settle an argument or help her out of a bind. She is a wild woman, so I really have no clue what to expect.

"Yes, sweet cheeks," she says in her trademark Southern drawl. "But I need you to pick Evangeline up for me."

"Leni?" My heart starts racing, wondering where she could be. She should've been in bed reading two hours ago. She is nothing if not a creature of habit. "Where is she?"

"Port Haven," she replies and I swear I can hear the smirk in her voice.

"What in the hell is she doing there? Not a place she would go ever, especially not alone, Nan."

"We might have been having a girls' day and ended up there. But I got a bit tired and she was talking to a nice feller at the bar. I didn't want to interrupt her nice time."

"You left her there alone?" I'm fuming. "With a strange man nonetheless?"

"Just for a bit. I was tired. Plus, I didn't want to put a damper on her evening. Chillin' with your grandmother isn't a great dating point." This conversation is pissing me off and I know I'm being irrational, but it is.

"I'll get her. But that was so irresponsible of you. What if something had happened to her?"

"You remember she's a full grown adult, don't you, Griffin?" she snaps at me. "She's not a child. She's gotta find happiness at some point. She can't wait forever."

"I am aware," I reply through gritted teeth before I take a deep breath to calm myself. It's not her that I'm upset with. She's just being her. "I'll go get her."

"Great, I'm just heading out. Poker night at Doris's house."

"It's after nine. Plus, I thought you left her there because you were tired."

"I was. I needed a catnap before poker night. Y'all don't wait up for me."

I'm already climbing in my truck when she hangs up the phone. Not even a goodbye, not that I expected one. That's her go to. Just says what she needs to then peace out.

The drive over the bridge to the bar doesn't take very long, but I spend the whole time telling myself not to overreact. I've kept my desire for her to myself for too long, not that I don't think that Leni hasn't caught me staring for a few seconds too long.

It's almost nine thirty by the time I arrive at the bar. I'm still in clothes from the remodel. Definitely not dressed for a night out on the town. I look around for my innocent redheaded Leni to be hiding in the corner with a book on her phone.

What I find is something much, much different. I approach the bar and immediately I see her. She's sitting there on the stool dead center of the bar. Her legs are crossed at the ankles and a short green dress has ridden up, exposing her thighs. She's turned on the stool facing some douchy guy in a suit. I take a step closer. I'm just behind them when his hand moves to her thigh and I see her tense up.

That's it, I'm done.

"Leni," I announce. "You ready to head back?"

"Griffin," she slurs, the asshole's hand still on her thigh. "Where did you come from?"

"I came by to take you home," I inform them both.

"I was already arranging for us to leave," the jerk says, grabbing Leni's hand. She looks down at their intertwined hands confused. "But thank you for the offer."

"I apologize, you seem to be confused. I'm taking her home," I inform him clearly, ready for him to make a scene.

"Griffin is such a nice man."

"You're friends with him?" the man asks her.

"He's my very best friend," she emphasizes, stumbling as she stands off the stool. "Guess what, friend, I think I might be a tad bit drunky. Have you ever had an apple martini? It's so tasty. He got me four, but I was a good girl and cut myself off then. He got me a fifth, but I gave it to the girl next to me."

The way she says friend irks me, but I can't deal with that. Right now, I gotta get her home safe and away from this ass who has to get a girl drunk to like him. I can't even think about what his plans were when he took her "home." Just the idea of him touching her has me verging on rage and that's not who I am.

"We appreciate your attempt to help"—and I stress the word help because I want him to know what I think his intentions were—"her home. But I live next door and I got this. But it seems you might need some help too. I can have the bartender call you a car."

"Umm." He seems confused, but I can tell he's gonna back off. "That's okay. My boys are here."

"Good. Leni, let's get you home." With my hand on her waist to make sure she doesn't fall, we head to the door. Thankfully the bar isn't too crowded off-season. We are steps away from getting out of here when she spins out of my hold and starts frantically looking around.

"Nan? Nan, wherrre are you?" She starts yelling over the music.

"Leni, she's at home."

"No, she's here with me. She went to the bathroom while I waited at the bar." She's still frantically searching around.

"Sweets, she left. She called me to come get you. Let's go home."

"My knight in shining armor." She throws her arms around me and we are standing flush together. "I always knew you would save me one day."

She lays her head on my chest. We're still standing here in a bar, but I just allow myself a moment to take in this feeling.

"Come on, let's get you home so you can sleep this off." I pull back from her and for the first time tonight I get a good look at the glory that is Evangeline Hughes.

She's always beautiful, but tonight she's so fucking sexy. I've never seen her like this. Even at our prom when she was all dressed up, she was gorgeous. But this, this look is pure sex. Tonight, she looks fucking hot.

With a small nod, she lets me lead her to my truck. I have to help her climb in, but I don't mind. I buckle her in and shut the door and head to the other side to get in the driver's seat. Our place isn't far yet somehow by the time the eight-minute drive is over, Leni is passed out.

I pull into my driveway and jump out to go around the truck to get her. I open the door and she still has the seat belt on because otherwise she would have fallen straight out of the cab. Somehow, I manage to unbuckle her and get her down out of the truck. She is still basically passed out. A few rambly words escape as I pick her up in my arms and carry her across the lawn to her place.

Thankfully, I have my own key. I manage to get the door open while still holding Leni, who seems perfectly comfortable with her head on my shoulder and her body in my arms. I relish in the feeling of her holding on to me, but I know this isn't real. Tomorrow she won't even remember how she got here.

"Okay, love, let's get you tucked in." I lay her on top of her white and rose printed quilt and head into the bathroom to look for something to help clean her face.

I'm about to grab some bar soap on a washcloth when I notice a packet on the sink labeled makeup remover. I pull out one of the wipes then glance back at the room where she's still passed out atop the covers. I remember just how different she looked tonight and decide it might be a two-wipe kind of night.

After making sure her face is clean, I attempt to get her to climb under the covers.

"Griffin," she half moans, half whispers and I beg my cock not to respond. Now is not the time for it to start getting ideas.

"Yes, babe," I call back to her.

"I gotta change. These aren't my clothes."

"Umm . . . they aren't?" I noted the sexy outfit she had on, it was impossible not to notice, but I wasn't going to say anything. At least not tonight. "What do you need?"

"Huh?" She blinks up at me, clearly already confused again. Alcohol is a bitch.

I decide to look for a nightgown to hand her before I head out, assuming that's what she's wanting. I root through a few drawers before finally finding one that looks like something a grandmother would wear.

I turn to hand it to her, expecting to see her passed out on the bed, but instead I'm greeted with the sight of her in a lacy black bra with the dress pooled around her waist as she sits on the bed.

This is going to be the only time in my life I think this but thank fuck she's too drunk to stand quickly. I do not need to see if the panties match the too fucking sexy bra she has on. Pushing the image of her out of my brain for now, I look up above her head, forcing myself to not take a second look at her as she shamelessly undresses. I pull the nightgown over her head just as I see her drop her bra on the floor.

"Fuck," I say to myself, knowing if I'd glanced down for just a second, I would have seen something I've only ever dreamed of seeing, but thankfully I know that wouldn't have been fair to her.

I take a few deep breaths, staring up at the ceiling before looking back down at Leni only to see her already completely passed out on top of her quilt. Her sexy outfit is discarded on the floor as if tonight had never happened. I look at my sweet, innocent, freckled face friend sleeping peacefully on the bed and silently ask myself if there is any way to pretend tonight didn't happen and I didn't see and feel what I saw and felt tonight.

I know the answer, but I decide to ignore my gut. She's never shown me any signs that she wants more from me than what we have. I won't risk her running from me because she doesn't feel the same way. I grab the crocheted blanket off her pink chair in the corner, cover her up, and quietly walk out of her house locking the door behind me as I go.

CHAPTER 11

Leni

I T'S BEEN A WEEK SINCE GRIFFIN PICKED ME UP FROM THE BAR and neither of us has initiated a conversation about it at all. Not that I remember everything I said or did that night. I've seen him several times, but we both just act like it didn't happen. I'm petrified that I completely embarrassed myself.

This is why I don't drink. I hate not being in complete control of mind and body. And I definitely hate not knowing if I confessed some very real very repressed feelings to a certain someone.

Work has been quiet lately, not that it's ever really booming with activity. I love how calm and peaceful my small old building is but days like today you could hear a pin drop in here.

The library is my safe space. It's a converted train station full of tiny rooms stuffed full of books. Some might think it's too crowded, old, and dusty, but I think it's perfect. Every now and then a notion goes around town that they want to build a newer bigger building and I know that would get more people into here, but the loss of charm would kill me.

Ever since I was a little girl this has been my favorite place in the world. I used to tell all the librarians here that one day I would be taking over for them. I think they expected I'd move on once I got out in the world, but there was never anything else I wanted to do or any place I wanted to be at more than my little library.

I'm checking in books that were dropped in the outdoor bin overnight when I notice the front door opening. In walks my new neighbor, Parker, book in her hand.

I like Parker. She's the kind of girl everyone notices when she enters the room. Her long blond hair is draped over her shoulders and somehow, she's rocking her basic waitressing uniform.

"Parker!" I say, excited to see her as she walks toward me. I come around from behind the desk to greet her.

"Hi, I was heading into work and wanted to drop off the book you sent Mikaela home with."

"Oh, great, did she like it?" I grab the book from her and set it down with the rest of the ones on the counter that I'm checking in.

"I think so. She's a hard girl to read sometimes, but she finished it in just a couple of days and that's saying a lot."

"Yay, let me get her the next in the series." I put down the stack of papers I was holding and point toward the young adult section, ready to lead her over there. Nothing makes me happier than when a young person first starts getting excited about reading.

"Sorry, I'm running super late. The sitter didn't show, and I had to beg your grandmother to watch Mikaela for a few hours until I can find a replacement at work. Can I grab it from you later?" she says in an apologetic tone.

"Not a problem at all. I'm actually getting off work in about an hour. How about I hang with her until your shift finishes? I have no plans and I can bring her the book. I'd love to hear what she thought about the first one."

"You sure?" she says hesitantly, her eyebrows raised. "I'd hate to impose."

"It's not a problem at all. I promise I didn't have anything going on tonight," I reassure her but leave out the fact that I never really have anything going on.

"You are a lifesaver. I owe you so much. Coffee next week? My treat," she tells me as I walk with her back across the small room toward the doorway.

"That would be great." I'm excited to spend more time with her. Both her and her niece are full of sass and I actually enjoy being around them.

"Mikaela is at your place, but if you want to go to mine since her stuff is all there, I left a key. There's dinner fixed in the fridge and she usually goes to bed by nine." Her words are coming fast, but I think I got it all. "I should be home shortly after that."

"I got it. Don't stress." With that she hurries to her beat-up car and I head back to finish the task at hand.

Just over an hour later, I arrive back at my place only to find Nan sitting on the porch with a large glass of white wine. I head inside and I'm confused as I find Mikaela standing over the sink doing the dishes. I put my stuff in my room and walk back out, trying to figure out what in the child labor is going on.

"Um, Nan, is there a reason there is a child doing chores while you lush it out here sitting on the porch?" I ask from the doorway separating the open living space from the porch.

"Chill, Peaches, I'm paying her." She casually sips her wine like that makes complete sense.

"Seriously, Nan, is doing your dishes so hard that you would pay a child just so you won't have to do them?"

"No, I heard her talking on the phone to her friend and she said she couldn't afford to go to the movies this weekend. Seeing as how her aunt is working her ass off and has to pay a babysitter, I figured she could use a little spending cash."

"Well . . . fine then. I guess that's nice of you. But drinking on the job?"

"What? I'm not getting paid, so therefore not a job, and she's not a baby." Another sip, with zero remorse. "Plus, I had a nightly wine daily while raising you and you turned out all right."

"Hmm, all right then." I give up. "I told Parker I would take over for you until she gets off work tonight. I'm here now, so you are set free."

"Nah," she says breezily while picking up a cracker off the plate in front of her. She takes a bite and turns to stare out into our yard like that's all the information I need.

I walk out onto the porch and over until I'm in her line of sight. "Whatcha mean nah?"

"I like the girl," she informs me, setting the glass down on the table and picking up a few of the grapes she has sitting out in a bowl. "She's got sass."

"No doubt there, but don't you have plans tonight?" Nan's a social bee, she has something going on almost every night of the week. I thought people slowed down as they got older, but she's only seemed to get busier and busier.

"Already canceled them. I just ordered us some Chinese food. Can you believe that she"—she points through the open door toward the kitchen—"has never had lo mein before? It's a travesty really."

"Oh, okay, I guess I'll go make me a salad or something then. I can take her back home after dinner and get her settled in bed."

"Sounds like a plan minus the salad. Never fear, I got you some orange chicken."

A huge grin covers my face. It's one of my favorite meals. After Mom died, we'd order Chinese food anytime either of us got down. That first year we had it delivered so much they knew what our order was just by seeing our number on the caller ID.

"Thanks, I love you. You know that, right?" I give her a peck on the cheek.

"Of course, Peaches. I'm very lovable and I love you too."

I walk back inside the house and talk to Mikaela while she finishes the dishes. We discuss the book and while her excitement level might not match mine, she seems to still be happy that I brought her the next in the series.

I spend the rest of the night hanging with the two of them, having more fun than I've had in a long time. We played Rummikub, ate too much food, and watched a couple of old episodes of *The Golden Girls*. Two hours later I can tell Mikaela is getting tired.

"I'm gonna take you home," I tell the yawning girl as I turn off the television. "Your aunt should be there in a few."

She doesn't fight me at all. Instead, she cleans up her place and says good night to Nan before we make the short walk across the street to her place.

Twenty minutes later she's brushed her teeth and washed her face and she's already passed out in her bed. I'm sitting on the couch in the living room reading the most delicious romance novel when Parker comes in through the door looking a bit worse for wear and exhausted compared to a few hours ago when I saw her before work.

"Hey," I whisper, not wanting to wake the sleeping girl in the room just around the corner.

"Hey, girl, don't stress," she says in a normal talking voice. "Once she's out she's out. Thank you and Helen so much for tonight."

"It wasn't a problem at all. We had a great time." I start to stand, ready to leave so she can get some rest, but she motions for me to sit back down.

"Yeah, Helen already texted me to inform me they're going shopping next week. Should I be worried?" she tells me as she plops down onto the recliner chair sitting across from me.

I can't help the snort that escapes, though I do attempt to cover it with a small cough, much to no avail. "No, she loves to shop, and they quickly hit it off. If she wants to hang with her and possibly buy her something, I say let her. It makes the old woman happy."

"Well, okay then, can't say I won't enjoy the free time. I'm still getting used to this whole being a caretaker thing. I absolutely love Mikaela, but I'm just really getting to know her myself and honestly some days it feels like I'm drowning."

"You're doing amazing and you have us now too. We're here for you anytime you need something."

"Thank you, it's nice to have a friend in town."

"Same, I don't have any girlfriends." Leaving off the fact that I've never really wanted any.

"What's the story on the fireman next door to you?" she casually asks as she wiggles around in the recliner until her legs are dangling off the side.

"Griffin? He's my best friend, has been ever since we were kids." *The best friend I want to see naked*, I think to myself.

"Just friends?" She raises her eyebrows and tilts down her chin as if to say she doesn't believe me.

"Yes." I giggle. "Just friends, that's all we've ever been. He's a really great guy. We should all hang out sometime." It's the truth, though I leave off the huge secret crush I've had on him since my teen years. That's my own special little secret. I've never told anyone, not even Nan.

I feel a yawn start to form and try to will it away, but it's no use. I'm exhausted and there is no hiding it.

"I better get home. I've got to be at work early tomorrow." I stand and gather up my bag and book.

"Yeah, Mikaela will have me up at the crack of dawn to get ready for school. But let's hang out soon." She follows me over to the front door, holding it open as I make my way onto the front porch.

"It's a plan. I had a good time with her and hanging with you for a few tonight. I left her with another book. Let me know when she's done, and I'll bring her another to switch it out. I know you're busy, so if you can't make it to the library it's no big deal."

"That's so sweet. Thank you, I will."

With another yawn, I make my way across the street, ready to climb into bed. Tomorrow Griffin comes for lunch and those are my favorite days. I plan on getting up early to catch up on all the work I missed by leaving a bit early today so that when he's there I can really enjoy hanging with him.

CHAPTER 12

Leni

A CRASH JERKS ME OUT OF THE MOST DELICIOUS DREAM. THE one I have whenever I'm feeling extra lonely but refuse to ever admit to out loud. The one where a certain firefighter kisses me passionately between the rows of books in my library. It's a dream I'll never acknowledge when the sun is up, but alone at night, I pray to have it whenever I close my eyes.

But right now, I don't have a second to fret over the loss of my precious dream. My heart is racing as I run from my room searching for the cause of the loud noise. It was a terrifying sound, one immediately followed by a strained cry that has pure panic coursing through my entire body.

"Nan?" I yell into the darkness. "Nan, where are you? Are you okay?"

My brain is running a mile a minute and yet I can't come up with one clear thought. Dashing into her room, I immediately notice the lamp missing from the table on the other side of the bed.

"Nan!" I scream out, rushing around the bed to confront my worst fears. There on the floor is the person I love most in this world. The one who's been there for me through the worst moments of my life. She's lying lifeless on her back, her eyes barely open. I fall to her side and with my ear to her mouth, I hear her strangled breath. She's still with me, thank goodness.

Everything in me wants to shut down and hide. It's how I've dealt with hard things in life for so long. But I can't let Nan down. I can't allow her to die because I didn't act fast enough.

I feel the tears pouring down my face and I jerk into motion, grabbing the phone off the nightstand and dialing 911. A silent prayer on my lips that she's going to be fine. I can't lose her. I won't survive it.

"Nine-one-one, how may I help you?" a woman's voice answers the phone with a calming tone. One that is probably supposed to ease my worry but instead has me frustrated. Who could be calm in an emergency?

"My grandmother. I heard a loud noise and found her on the floor unconscious. She's breathing but just barely. Please hurry." I keep checking to make sure she's breathing while forcing myself to stay focused on the call at the same time.

"Okay, ma'am. I'm sending paramedics right away. We have your address and they will be there shortly."

"I don't know what I'm doing." I'm close to hysterics and I can't get my emotions under control. I need to focus. To do something. I need to save her.

"It's okay, I'm here to help you. I'll talk you through everything until the paramedics arrive."

Before the operator can walk me through CPR instructions, I hear the front door open with a bang.

"Leni, Leni. Please, please be okay, Leni." I hear him yell out from the front of the house. Relief floods over me. He'll fix this. He's a firefighter. He can save her and make it all better.

"Griffin, in here. It's Nan!" I yell from the floor in her room where I'm still sitting with her head in my lap.

He's in here in a flash, on his knees beside Nan. I'm frozen, still watching him try to save her life. "I heard the call on my radio."

Between breaths into her mouth, he turns to me. "Ambulance should be here in a minute. Go meet them up front. Tell them I'm here doing CPR for a fall." She's still not awake. He's pushing on her chest and breathing into her mouth and she's still not waking up.

"I can't, Griffin, I can't. This isn't real." I move to the side so I'm not in the way, but I can't get my feet to take me out of her room. What if something happened and I wasn't here, or she comes to and doesn't see me?

"Leni, I love you and I know you're freaking out. But right now, you need to be brave and put it aside. Go get them and when they get here, I'll be here for you. When she's safe you can fall apart, but until then you need to pull it all together. For Helen."

Silently, I turn out of the bedroom and reach the front of the house where the door is still wide open from when he arrived. I'm barely out the door before I see the flashing lights coming down our small street. I'm running on autopilot as I lead them in and watch them put her on a stretcher and wheel her into the ambulance.

The whole thing only took minutes, but time for me is frozen and it feels like hours. I'm on the porch as they finish getting her loaded. I feel warm arms grab me from behind and warm breath in my ear.

"Breathe, Leni, breathe. Go ride with her. Be there for her. She might not be awake, but she'll know you're there. I'll follow in my truck."

"Tell me she's gonna make it. Griffin, tell me, I need to hear it."

"Shh. We can talk at the hospital." He pulls his hoodie off and hands it over to me. "Put this on. It's going to be cold in there and I have a feeling you're going to want the coverage."

I look down and realize I'm in my small black sleep shorts and the thinnest tank top I own. Thank goodness for him; he's always been my savior. Even back when I didn't want one.

"Okay, thank you." I pull the large oversized sweatshirt over my head and allow myself one second to relish in the manly scent before I take off and jump into the back of the ambulance.

The ride to the hospital was the most scared I've ever been. The paramedics acted quickly, hooking her up to machines and getting an IV in place. I cowered in the corner in my seat, petrified of interfering and messing something up.

We arrive at the hospital fifteen minutes later. Why on earth do we live so far from a hospital? In a flash, the paramedics pull the gurney with Nan on it out of the ambulance and rush her into the back of the emergency room.

"Ma'am," a soft voice calls to me. I turn and see a nurse, who can't be older than twenty, motioning for me to follow her. "I'll take you to the waiting room and the doctors will be out as soon as they have an update for you."

I nod, not knowing what words to say. I follow behind her silently as we walk through a maze of corridors until we go through two large swinging doors that lead to a mostly empty waiting room. In the corner, I spot my Griffin. There waiting for me, like he always is.

He's up and with me in seconds, his arms grabbing my waist as all the strength I've been trying to hold onto since I found her on the floor melts out of my body. I have nothing left to give as I place the life of the only family I have left into the hands of the doctors and nurses.

It's been two hours since they deposited me in the waiting room and rushed Nan off. Not once during that entire time has Griffin left me or let go of my hand. Other than a few updates that they were still working on her from the nurse I have no clue how she's doing.

It's past one in the morning when an older doctor in a long white coat and a name badge that reads 'Dr. Johnson' walks over to where we are sitting in the waiting room. I stand to talk to him, willing my weak legs to hold me up. Griffin is by my side, his arm wrapped around my waist. A simple comfort, but one I desperately need to hold me up.

"Ms. Hughes?" he says out loud, not yet looking up from the chart.

"Yes, that's me," I respond, trying to read his face.

"Your grandmother Helen had a transient ischemic attack. It's more commonly called a mini-stroke. She's very lucky you were there."

"She's okay?" I ask flatly. Her being alive is all I need to hear right now.

"She's not out of the woods, but we have her stable at the moment."

I feel the relief flow through my body.

"When she fell, she fractured her hip."

I gasp. I knew she fell hard enough to knock her out, but I still wasn't prepared for this.

"Is she going to be able to recover?" Griffin asks from beside me.

"She will need surgery to set her hip but before then we have to make sure she's strong enough to be put under anesthesia. Hopefully we will know more later today."

I can only nod as the tears start to fall, knowing she's in pain and probably terrified.

"Are you aware that your grandmother has a DNR in place?"

Closing my eyes, I take in a deep breath before I reopen them. "Yes, sir," I tell the doctor standing in front of me. After everything we went through with Mom, Nan had a very frank conversation with me when I was younger. She refuses to live her life hooked up to machines.

I'm a smart woman. I know what's coming, but I don't think I could ever be ready for what comes next. Years ago, long after Mom had passed and I'd matured into a teenager, Nan let me know that after watching her daughter struggle for years she couldn't stand for that to happen to me and that she had set up a do not resuscitate order. It'd torn me up and at the time I'd done everything I could to convince her to undo it.

"Tonight, she's stable and we are giving her oxygen as needed. She's on a bunch of meds for pain and to help her sleep. We don't anticipate anything going wrong, we just need to make sure you are aware of the situation before we proceed." Once again, I just nod, feeling like a child all over again. "Tomorrow you'll sit down with the doctors and surgeons and they will tell you everything you need to know about stroke recovery and what will happen before her surgery."

"Can I see her?" I finally find my voice.

"Of course, but just one visitor at a time," the doctor tells me with an apologetic smile.

I look at Griffin to make sure he's okay.

"I'll be here when you get out. Don't worry, go be with her," he reassures me as he sits back down in the hard plastic chair with a probably two-year-old copy of *Good Housekeeping* ready for a long night.

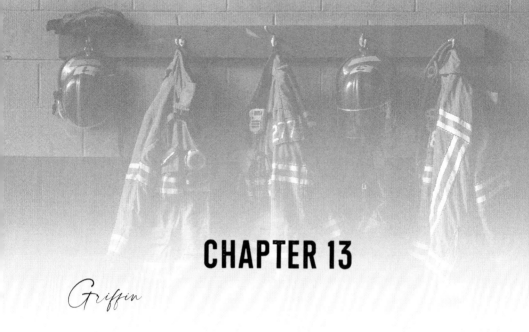

CHAPTER 13

Griffin

I'M NOT SURE WHEN I FELL ASLEEP IN THE SMALL PLASTIC CHAIR in the waiting room, but I awoke to Leni standing over me, holding two cups of coffee.

"Morning," I say, stretching my arms out wide. She's exhausted, I can tell. I grab a cup of coffee and stand to face her. "Did you get any sleep?"

"No, not really. But Doris is here now and asked if she could stay there for a few hours." Doris has been Helen's best friend for as long as I can remember, even before Leni moved to town. I remember the two of them drinking wine and cat-calling men jogging on the street when I was just a small kid. Mom would always giggle and say she wanted to be just like them when she got old.

"Did the doctors come in?" I stand and take a sip of the burnt coffee.

"Yeah, they say she's stable and doing as well as expected. She's wo-ken up a bit, but is very groggy and mostly sleeping. Her hip surgery is probably going to be in a day or two and if things go well, she'll be here for a few more days after that before going to a rehabilitation home for recovery."

"That's good that she woke up, right?"

"Yeah, but it's still so scary, Griffin, what if she has another episode? What if there are long-term problems from the stroke?" she says, tearing up for the millionth time tonight. My heart is breaking and all I want to do is make everything better for her. But I can't fix this and it's killing me.

"Why don't you let me drive you home." I put the coffee cup down on the table and take her cup to set on the table as well. I pull her into my arms and feel her instantly relax into me. "Let me take care of you."

That's all I ever want to do, take care and protect her like she's the most precious thing in the world because to me she is.

"Huh?" She snaps out of her blank stare and looks up into my eyes. "Yeah, that's probably a good idea. Sleep would be good."

"I'll go talk to the nurse and see what they need from us and then we'll get you home for a hot shower and some sleep. We'll come back here in a few hours when Doris's heading home."

It's five-thirty in the morning and we've been at the hospital for hours. She's got to be tired and hungry. I haven't had any dinner. I was just getting off shift when I heard the call on the way home.

She was desperate and panicked when they arrived at the hospital and since then she's barely said a dozen words other than when she's getting updates from the staff.

Once I confirm the nurses have all the information they need, I lead Leni out to my truck. I can tell it hasn't truly hit her that Helen will be in recovery for a while, or even what the full dangers of the surgeries that are coming will be. Helen's the only family she has left, and they are as close as two people can be. I don't know anyone else who is that happy and content to be living with their grandmother at twenty-seven years old.

After the short drive home, I pull into her driveway. As if on auto-pilot she opens the door and steps out without uttering a single word. She's clutching her keys as she takes slow, deliberate steps toward the front porch.

My heart is aching knowing I can't take away her pain. All I can do is try to make the night easier for her. It's killing me watching her go through this, just like when her mom died all those years ago.

"Why don't you go inside and get a shower and put some clean clothes on. I'll run down the street to the twenty-four-hour diner and grab us something to eat."

"Sure, I can do that." She pauses in front of the porch. I watch her from the side of my truck as she walks slowly up the three stairs leading to the porch. She walks up to the front door, keys in her hands. After a minute or two standing there, she opens the door, but she doesn't budge from her spot on the porch.

It's not fair, she's been through too much in her life. I don't know how to take some of the burden away, but if I could carry it for her, I'd take it all. I wait for her to make a move to go inside the house.

She's not going in. Instead, she's just staring at the front door wide open, but yet she stands completely frozen. Shit, I'm an asshole. I shouldn't have sent her up there alone, after watching her grandmother almost die in there last night. I quickly head up the stairs and through the door onto the screened in porch.

Standing right behind her, I say nothing. I want her to do what she wants in this moment. I place my hand on her shoulder and immediately she turns toward me. I place an innocent kiss on her forehead, and she leans into me. I want to tell her how much I love her. I want to tell her how it's all going to be okay. I want to tell her she's not alone. But I know right now she won't hear any of it.

I'll be here by her side. She won't have to handle any of this alone. Putting both my arms around her waist, she falls into me. Grabbing her hand, I walk us over to the porch swing and we sit in silence. Her whole body falling onto mine, her head resting on my shoulder like I'm the only one who could possibly keep her from falling apart right now. I drown in the sounds of her breathing. Several minutes pass with neither of us talking. Finally, I sit up straight to look into her deep green eyes only to see them full of the tears she's desperately trying to keep at bay.

"Leni, are you okay? Talk to me. Please talk to me." I'm begging, but I'm so desperate for an inkling of what's going on inside her head so I can help her. All I want right now is to make it better.

She stares just past me and for several minutes I think she's not going to say anything. But still, patiently I wait for her to be ready.

"I can't go in. I opened the door, but my feet just wouldn't allow me inside that house. For years it's been my sanctuary from the chaotic world, but so much loss has happened in there and I just can't go inside. I'm not ready. It feels like I might never be ready."

I'm sure for anyone else this would seem like an overreaction. But this is where she lost her mom and then having to see her only other relative almost fall to the same fate in the house would of course be too much.

"Oh, Leni." I rise from the porch swing and pull her up to standing. Holding both her hands, I keep full eye contact so that she hears the next words that come out of my mouth. "Come home with me. You know you are always welcome there. Come stay a night, a week, a month."

A lifetime. I add in my head. But those aren't words I can say to her. Our friendship is all she has left, and I can't risk hurting her more by taking the chance on losing that too.

"Okay," she whispers into the night air.

I grab her hand, making a small stop at the truck to turn it off and lock it before I lead her over the small patch of grass that separates her place from mine. Once we are inside, she follows me to the master bedroom, and I grab one of my gym shirts and a pair of my boxer briefs. With her still on my heels, not saying a word, I turn the shower on for her.

"Take a shower and get the smell of the hospital off of you. You'll sleep better if you do. I'll run to the diner and get us some food before you go to sleep."

Nodding, she takes the clothes out of my hands and walks into the bathroom, shutting the door behind her.

Luckily, I have the diner's number in my phone and give them a call on the way to save time. By the time I'm there the food is ready.

"Thanks, Jim." Jim's owned the diner for as long as I can remember.

"No problem, Griffin. Helen's a good woman and I know poor Evangeline is out of her mind with worry. After all she went through with her momma."

"News travels fast in a small town, huh," I say with a smirk, not surprised at all at how quickly the gossip train works around here.

"Yeah, well, Susan was on duty over at County General and she called."

Susan is Jim's wife and a nurse at the hospital. I figured we'd have at least until morning before the news started to spread, but I should have known better.

"Tell Evangeline we're so sorry. Meal's on us tonight." He hands the bag over and I can already see a few pieces of pie on top I didn't order. I know a lot of people love living in the big cities, but I can't imagine living somewhere where the whole town didn't rally together when one of its residents needs it.

"Thanks, man. I will tell her. I better get out of here and get back to her. I hated leaving her all alone."

My mind is on Leni the whole ride home. I shouldn't have left her. I have a bad feeling it was the wrong move and I regretted it as soon as I got to the diner, but she needs some sustenance and my fridge is empty.

Holding the bags of food in one hand, I unlock my front door and walk into the eerily silent house.

"Leni, I'm back with all your favorites," I call out, but still, I hear nothing. Abandoning the bags on the coffee table, I walk back to my room and hear the shower still running.

"You in there?" I call out while knocking on the door. Something doesn't feel right and after several seconds pass with no answer I decide to open the bathroom door to check on her.

"Leni," I call through the door. "Are you doing okay?"

I hear her small sobs through the sound of water, but she doesn't say anything.

Creeping the door open, I call out once more, "Leni, I'm worried. Please let me know if you're okay."

I encounter panicked people every day at work and have to stay calm in some harrowing situations. But nothing can prepare me for the intense emotions boiling inside me watching my best friend struggle to cope.

A small sniffle comes from the shower. "Physically yeah," she says softly. "But emotionally? I just don't know, Griffin." Her voice is weak, and I know she's exhausted.

Pain sears through my heart knowing I can't instantly fix this.

"Do you want me to help you?" I ask from the other side of the shower curtain.

"Yes." She's tired and worn out, I convince myself. Some rest will do her some good.

I don't know if she's talking about the big picture of overcoming yet another tragedy in life. Or if she's talking about the immediate need of getting up and dressed, but I don't overthink any of it. Instead, I slowly pull the curtain back and grab a towel off the wall.

She's sitting on the bottom of the bath curled up into herself, her head resting on her legs. She looks so small and frail, but I need to remind her and me that she isn't fragile. She's sassy and witty and puts me in my place whenever I need it. But we'll get there. Tonight I just need to be the shoulders she leans on.

I fall to my knees in front of this beautiful, innocent, and tormented angel, taking the towel with me to cover her. The freezing cold water is still pouring onto my back, soaking my clothes, but I don't care. I just move quickly to make sure she isn't uncomfortable with me.

Several moments pass of me holding her there on the floor of the shower before she finally looks up and makes eye contact with me.

"Thank you," she says, her green eyes staring deep into mine.

Despite the freezing shower and the emotional night we just had, I can't help but look from her eyes down to her plump lips.

God, I would kill to taste them just once. I shouldn't be having those thoughts right now. I'm mentally berating myself when she goes and lets the tip of her tongue glide over her bottom lip.

If I didn't know better, I would swear she wants me to kiss her too, but there's no way that's true. Even if there was a tiny sliver of her that wants that right now it's just a distraction from life and I won't be that. Not from the one girl I've always wanted.

Breaking the silence in the room, I let out a small cough and then go and turn the shower off. I grab a clean dry towel from the bar next to the shower and hold it up for her. She stands while holding the wet towel in place with one hand and grabs the dry one with her free hand.

"I'll give you a minute to get dressed, but I'm not leaving again. I promise." I reassure her before leaving the bathroom. Once the door is shut, I let out the sigh I've been holding in while running my hands through my hair.

Hastily, I quickly grab myself some clean sweatpants and take a fast shower in the guest bathroom. When I return to my room to see if she wants to eat, I find Leni sitting on the bottom of the bed yawning.

"You take my bed. I'll stay on the couch." There are two other bedrooms in the house but seeing as I live alone neither is guest ready. One I turned into a gym and there's a bed in the other one for when my parents visit, but I haven't gotten around to washing the sheets since they were here visiting last.

"Thanks." She climbs up the bed and crawls under the covers. I swear I hear her take an inhale of my pillow and even though I know I have no right to and it's completely inappropriate right now I can't help the small smile that crosses my lips at the thought of her enjoying my scent. It's barbaric and probably not what she was doing at all, but try to tell that to my lips right now. They have a mind of their own as the tips of them won't stop tilting upward.

I make my bed on the couch out in the living room and settle in, ready to watch some old reruns on the TV once Leni is in bed. About fifteen minutes pass and I'm almost completely passed out when I hear her voice.

"Griffin," she softly calls out to me.

"Yes, love," I say back without even thinking as I walk back into my room and get my first full glance of her lying in my bed, on my sheets, wrapped up like she belongs there.

"Will you stay in here with me? I can't sleep. My mind is racing a million miles an hour and when I'm with you I just feel calmer."

"Leni, I'd do anything for you." Without thinking I lie down next to the woman I love.

CHAPTER 14

Leni

I WAKE HAVING SLEPT HARDER THAN I EVER HAVE. THE EMOTIONAL rollercoaster I went on last night must have been exhausting for me to sleep all night with everything that's on my mind right now.

Before my eyes are even open, I notice my arms and legs are wrapped around someone, not just someone, a very specific someone: Griffin. I'm clinging to his hard-chiseled body like it's the raft in the Titanic and I'm Rose.

Flashes of begging him to stay with me last night crash into my memory and I start to move my body back to my side of the bed.

"Stop overthinking." I hear his sleepy voice mumble from beneath the covers. "It's only been a few hours, go back to sleep. We'll head over to the hospital soon."

Stop overthinking? Does he honestly believe that's possible at this moment in time? Between Nan almost dying and my sleep-induced brain deciding last night was the time to push my body up against his, there's more than ever to overthink about.

"I should have stayed there with her. I could have stayed."

"You heard Doris last night. She wanted to stay and insisted you get some rest. We can all take turns helping out. You have to let some of the weight go. Plus, I heard your phone dinging non-stop with her constant updates."

Doris and Nan have been friends since they were five and even married a pair of brothers in a joint ceremony when they were twenty. Sadly, Nan lost her husband, my grandfather, only two months after my mom was born and she never remarried. Heck, I'm not even sure she ever dated after losing him.

But I can't tell him that isn't what I was overthinking. I can't admit my embarrassment over how I crawled and clung to him as if my life depended on it. And I definitely can't tell him how sad I was to unlatch my body from his.

Still, it's my own policy to never lie, so instead of responding to him, I climb out of bed and head into the bathroom to take a hot shower and try to wash the guilt of lusting over Griffin when I should have all my thoughts and energy be directed to Nan's recovery.

He's always had a way of getting me out of the dark and into the light. It's addicting. But today I have something else bigger to focus on.

Fifteen minutes later I'm squeaky clean and ready to tackle the day when I realize my big mistake. I emerge from the bathroom, praying he's left his room because clearly my mind was elsewhere when I went in here since I didn't even bother to bring any clean clothes with me.

No such luck, he's sitting up in bed with his glasses on and a magazine in his hands.

Crap!

"Sweatpants are in the bottom drawer and T-shirts top left," he tells me without even looking up from his magazine. Damn, a man reading is a sexy sight and those glasses only add to the pure heat brewing inside me. *Head in the game, Leni, not in the gutter. Now is not the time to lust over him.*

"Thanks." I rush to grab them and get back into the bathroom before he looks up and gets a glimpse of my bare ass.

Once dressed, I turn down an offer for breakfast from Griffin, opting instead to head next door to get some of my clothes and feed Toby.

The empty house during the day is a lot less daunting, but the idea of being here without Nan is still in the back of my head. I don't know what I'll do tonight, but I'm not going to think about that now if I can help it. I'll just have to cross that bridge when it's time.

It's around seven-thirty when Griffin walks through the front door, a travel mug of coffee in each hand. I'm sitting at the table, staring at the list I've been making in front of me of any and everything Nan might need for the next few days.

The doctors messaged me this morning that she was stable enough to have her surgery today. I'll get more details when I get to the hospital, but I need to be prepared for a long day of waiting around.

"You ready?" he calls out after letting himself in. "I can take you to the hospital before I head into work. I messaged Doris to let her know you were coming during the day. She said she would go freshen up and run some errands but be there tonight again. I called Linda and she's going to make sure your shifts are covered this week. News is spreading in town and she said they already got volunteers lined up."

"Oh, thank you. Yeah, let me just grab Nan's stuff. Did Doris say if she was awake yet?"

"Not yet, but she is showing signs of starting to stir. They gave her meds last night to help her sleep, so it's no surprise she hasn't woken up yet."

I rush to get to the hospital, not wanting to miss the doctors' rounds. I've been sitting silently by Nan's bedside for two hours and they just left. Her surgery is scheduled, and everything is ready to go.

I sit and wait, praying she will open her eyes and say something smartassy to me. Last night was the worst night I've had since losing Momma and I'm not ready to lose her too. I never will be. I try to distract myself by diving headfirst into a fun, romantic comedy book, but even that isn't working. Setting the book down, I pick up my phone and open my text messages with Griffin.

ME: You know I'm having a bad day when I can't even read a book.

GRIFFIN: She doing okay?

ME: As good as they expect. Surgery is scheduled. I never realized how much I still feel like a child until I almost lost her. I think I actually thought I would live with her forever.

GRIFFIN: You're definitely an adult. Maybe it's time you move out. Once she's back.

ME: Yeah, I was sitting here thinking that myself. Especially since I can't even bring myself to stay in my own house.

GRIFFIN: Hey, no complaints from me. I liked having you with me last night.

ME: Yeah, like when we were younger and would camp out in the backyard.

GRIFFIN: Something like that. I got to go. Captain just walked in. I'll see you tonight. I brought some of your clothes over to my place. No rush on leaving, okay?

ME: Okay. Thank you.

I feel better after talking with him, but then again, I always do. Picking my book back up, I give reading another go, and I'm quickly lost to the romantic and silly world the author has created.

I'm just getting to the good part, the exciting first kiss. It's my favorite part of romance novels. I love how full of hope and promise those moments are. This kiss did not disappoint, I'm so lost to the words and the magic world books put me in I don't even notice when Nan's eyes open.

"Hi." I hear a whisper of her voice and I jump up, dropping the book on the floor.

"Oh. My. God, Nan, you're awake." I rush to her bedside and immediately push the nurse button so they can come check on her.

"I am, Peaches, I'm here, not leaving you yet," she raspily says with a laugh and a cough. A groan escapes her as she attempts to sit more upright.

"Not funny," I tell her while I help her adjust the bed before I buzz the nurses' station to check to make sure they are on their way before Nan hurts herself. "Let me help you. You're going to hurt yourself if you keep moving around. How are you feeling?"

"Not my best." She looks around, taking in the room and all the machines hooked up to her. "How you holding up?"

Leave it to Nan to worry about me when she almost died. Why do I have to be this fragile? Everyone knows it. I can be strong. I need to be strong. I decide against telling her that I couldn't stay at our place last night. As long as she doesn't ask it's not a lie.

"I'm gonna be fine," I say, attempting to sound confident even though I'm anything but. "We are going to be fine."

"Fuck yeah, we are. I got tons more trouble to cause before y'all get rid of me." She smiles, but I see the pain in her eyes, and it breaks me a bit to see her stuck in that bed.

"Hilarious, Nan, really hilarious."

"Speaking of trouble," she says, motioning with her head to the young male nurse who just walked into her room.

"Be good," I tell her under my breath.

"Never," she replies with a wink.

It's not long before she's back asleep. She's still groggy from the sleeping meds they gave her to help make sure the pain isn't constantly waking her.

It's nine at night by the time Griffin picks me up to take me home. I probably should've driven myself here, but I liked him bringing me. Despite the two of us spending most of our free time together I never get tired of him.

After a long day of him working and me being at the hospital both of us are exhausted. We don't even have a conversation about where I'm going or what we're doing. We both stumble into his place and change into comfy clothes.

It's cold this time of the year on the coast and thankfully Griffin pulled some soup I froze for him a few weeks ago out this morning and threw it in the crockpot.

"I'll get the food, you pick out the show," he says to me as we head into the house.

"Oh, yeah, okay." I head into the living room to sit on the couch to watch TV like we always do. I slump onto the couch, not even turning anything on.

A couple of minutes later Griffin walks in with two bowls and gets one look at me lying on the couch overthinking life and declares, "Never mind, change of plans. We need a night out. We've had a hell of a week and I think we need to unwind."

"Going out? Really? You do know I don't do that on a good week, don't you?" It's like he's never met me before.

"I know, but I think a distraction is what you and I both need. Now get some shoes on and let's head out."

"You know what?" I stand up and pull my tangled hair up into a messy bun. "That sounds like a great idea. Give me five minutes and I'll be ready."

Twenty minutes later we pull into the drive-thru of the only fast food place in our town. He orders us some burgers, fries, and sweet teas and he drives us over the bridge toward the ocean. We pull into the public parking lot on the beach and he grabs us a couple of blankets from the back of the truck. We head out onto the path toward the beach. At the end of the path there's a gazebo I know too well. It's cold but calm tonight, perfect for a fall picnic.

Griffin leads the way with me right behind him. As soon as we get there, he gets to work, laying some blankets over the dirty benches under the gazebo for us to sit on.

"This is one of my favorite spots," I tell him as I sit down while he gets to work pulling the food out for us.

"I know. You told me a while back when we came here to look for shells," he says, a proud smile on his face.

"I can't believe you remembered. It's so peaceful here this time of year." I shove a fry in my mouth, not realizing until the smell hits my nose just how hungry I am.

"I remember everything you tell me. Don't you know that by now?"

I just smile before taking a bite of my burger. I wish I knew what he was thinking, what he wants from me right now. But I'll settle for just knowing that when I'm in need he's always going to be here for me.

"Thank you for this. I haven't been anywhere but home, the hospital, and work since Nan got hurt. This is just what I needed."

I barely remember mentioning once that when I would think about my mom and get down, I'd come here with my Kindle at night and read while listening to the sound of the ocean. It calms and soothes me. Just makes me all around happier. The fact that he remembered me telling him all that one time chokes me up just a bit. He really is a great guy. One I never want to not have in my life.

We finish eating in silence and after he stands to go throw away the trash in the can outside the gazebo, I think he's going to suggest going home. After all, it's late and we both have to get up early. But he surprises me. He comes back and sits beside me on the bench, content to just be with me here. I lay my head down in his lap and close my eyes to listen to the sound of the waves.

"I don't deserve you," I quietly tell him, a small shiver in my voice.

He takes that moment to cover me with the extra blanket before telling me, "You deserve everything in life."

We sit here listening to the sounds of the water until I start to doze off. Anyone else would probably be bored just sitting silently late into the night, but I can't imagine a better way to end this stressful day.

The rest of the week goes by much the same. Nan's surgery is successful, and she came through wonderfully. She's going to be bed-bound for a while and then needs intensive physical therapy before she can move around on her own, but at least she's alive and able to fight through.

There doesn't seem to be any long-term problems from the mini-stroke she had, but the doctors did warn us this might not be the only one she has, and she will need to be under the care of a neurologist.

I'm still mentally worn out, but for the first time since that awful night I feel like things might actually be okay.

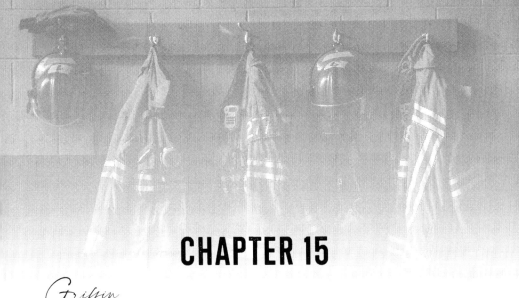

CHAPTER 15

Griffin

"**Y**OU'RE STILL DOWN TO HEAD TO THE BAR TONIGHT?" Jack asks as we both finish putting our gear away. We both have the next two days off and I know I for one am in desperate need of a break.

"Definitely, Leni is at the hospital tonight with her grandmother, so I have zero plans," I tell him as we head to the parking lot toward our cars.

"Yeah." Jack rakes his hands through his hair. "Noticed you've been spending even more time with your girl than normal."

I ignore him, opting instead to say bye to the rest of the guys who are hanging outside by the grill. Before he can say anything else, I climb in my truck and start to head over to the only bar in our small town. There are a few across the bridge but only one small local dive bar on this side.

Once I get there I walk in and I'm glad to see it's a slow night. I'm not in the mood for a big crowd. Jack is right behind me and I've just finished ordering my beer when he sits down on the bar stool next to me.

"Been a long time since we've gone out," I say as Mike, the bartender, puts the beers down in front of us. I went ahead and ordered him one too and by the size of the gulp he just took it's clear he needs it.

"Yeah, life is." He pauses to take another sip. "Hectic to say the least. Marriage and a kid in less than a year can wear a man out."

"I bet. Speaking of, how are Shelby and Ava? Been a while since I've gotten to see them. I bet she's growing like crazy."

"She is. Shelby took her to her parents' for a visit. They'll probably be back in a few weeks." His face falls as he tells me they are gone.

"Everything all right?" I ask while I finally take a sip of my own beer.

"Yeah. It's just a lot for her, you know. Our schedule is a lot for someone who isn't used to it. We'd barely dated before we got married and she got pregnant. Ya know?"

Damn. I've noticed he's seemed down lately. He's always been outgoing and a bit loud and he's been quiet and reserved for a while now. It's part of why I asked him to come out tonight. Seemed like he needed it. But now I feel like a pretty shit friend. I've been so wrapped up in my own life that I didn't even notice how much he was struggling.

"Well, hi, Griff," Laurie Vanderson says while putting her arms around my neck from behind.

Fucking hell. Laurie and I have a very brief, very unmemorable past from way back in the days just after high school. We spent some time together that first year after Leni left for college. It wasn't anything special and we never really dated, but I always thought that she might want more.

I've become an expert at dodging her, though luckily, she stays away whenever Leni is with me. But I'm exhausted and off my game and I let her sneak up on me tonight.

"Hi, Laurie, how've you been?" I ask out of politeness as I remove her arms from around me. I take a sip of my beer as she goes on and on about some drama she's having with some of the other girls we went to school with.

I swear around here if you don't get out you get stuck. I guess that makes me stuck. It's a sobering thought, one that has me downing the rest of my beer. Jack already has another round coming for us before I can even flag down the bartender.

Pushing mine in front of me, we both pick them up at the same time, all the while Laurie is still rambling. Apparently, she doesn't need an active audience in order for her to carry on a conversation.

"Cheers," I say, bumping his glass as we both down our second of the night. Laurie must finally get fed up with being ignored because she waves down some random man I don't recognize at the other end of the bar and walks off with barely a wave goodbye.

"Still can't believe you willingly spent time with her. Don't think she ever stops talking."

"Yeah, that was just one of the many reasons I stopped spending time with her."

"That and your undying love for a certain redhead."

"There is that too." I don't even deny it. We've had many a drunken night where I've unloaded on him over the years. But tonight, unlike all those I have a bit of hope that it won't be just unrequited love.

One of these days I'm gonna work up the nerve to make a move other than just holding her in my bed every morning while begging my erection to go away before she notices I can barely control myself when she's near. Her skittish ways have always kept me at bay, but I don't know how much longer I can last with her in my house and not telling her exactly how I feel.

I'm honestly not even sure I'll be able to sleep tonight without the smell of her peach shampoo next to me. It's the first night since Helen went into the hospital that Doris couldn't stay with her. I think Leni was excited to have a girls' night with her even if it's in the hospital. She packed a board game and a DVD player so they could watch movies.

"Where do Shelby's parents live?" I ask, hoping it's not far. I don't know her well, but if he loves her, I hope she's not going to be gone long.

"In the Raleigh area now. They used to live in Texas but moved to North Carolina when she was a teenager. She's got a bunch of clients there and her parents offered to help with Ava for a bit while she worked."

"Oh, is she gonna be gone a while?" I don't say it, but it doesn't sound like a quick visit.

"Not sure. I'm gonna drive up for the day tomorrow to see Ava."

"And Shelby?" I ask. I need to stop being so nosy, but he needs a friend. Not letting anything out only builds the tension.

"Yeah, after she finishes working. She's got a big client there and is working every day to get it finished. It's a big payout and she thinks we really need it."

We don't make a ton of money in our job, but that's not why we do it. Still, I always thought we made plenty for a good life. I wonder if Leni thinks the same. Who am I kidding, she's not the sort of girl who places value on material things. Money has never been a motivator in her life.

Changing the subject, I ask him about his plans with Ava tomorrow. Apparently, there's a big kids' museum not far from where his in-laws live and he's taking her there. I don't mention she's probably too young to care about any of that, plus I'm pretty sure from the way he's talking about it that it's him who's excited for the life-sized dinosaur exhibit they have there.

An hour later we've finished our second beers and we're both ready to call it a night. Long gone are the days of staying out late. Nowadays I'd prefer to be hanging out watching a movie so much more than hitting the bars.

I fully expect to pass out right away. I worked a long day and it was exhausting. But two hours of me staring at the ceiling pass and I cannot fall asleep. I turn the lamp on and sit up in my bed. I pull out my phone and open up my text messages.

ME: You awake?

It's going on eleven. I don't fully expect a response. She's either passed out in an uncomfortable chair, watching a movie, or reading a book. Unlike most other girls in their twenties, she's barely ever on her phone. Half the time she doesn't notice my text messages until hours later.

LENI: I am, but shouldn't you be sleeping by now? Normally after a long shift you've fallen asleep by ten.

ME: Haha, it's too quiet in here.

LENI: You know there's this thing that was invented a little while back called a television. Word on the street is it makes noise.

ME: Yeah, but I prefer the cute snores I've gotten used to hearing.

She's quiet. Ten minutes pass with no response.
Shit.
My flirting went too far.

LENI: Sorry, the nurse came in. And I prefer sleeping in your bed so much more than this uncomfortable recliner chair. I'm missing it so much right now.

I thought I scared her off. But she's still with me and she didn't change the subject. I decide to push a little further. I pray it doesn't backfire on me, but I'm so worked up thinking about her and her soft body I just can't help but to see if she's on the same page.

ME: The bed feels too big. I miss you.

Again, she's quiet and my mind starts to wonder if I've gone too far. Pushed her too fast. I've wanted her for so long and having her in my grasp makes pacing myself almost impossible. But as strong as a woman as she is, she's also so easily scared.

LENI: It's odd, I've only ever really slept alone but I miss you too.

I can feel my heart racing, desperately needing her. This is more than I ever dreamed I'd get from her. I should be resigned to just know I get to spend this time so close to her when she's here with me. But I can't settle for what I have when everything I've ever wanted is finally within reach.

> ME: Try to get some sleep. I'm off tomorrow. Wanna get breakfast?
>
> LENI: OMG. I'm desperate for some grits. The Breakfast Joint at ten sounds good. Doctors make rounds early so I should be able to make it by then. I'm hoping they are going to let her leave the hospital in the next day or so.
>
> ME: It's a plan. See you then.

I wake too early for it to be my day off. My body is just not conditioned to sleeping in like it could back in my early twenties when I had no real responsibilities. I roll to the other side of the bed and instantly her scent hits me. It's as if she washed the pillowcase in her shampoo.

My cock reacts immediately. It's unbearably hard. I don't think I'll ever be able to smell peaches again without at least rocking a semi. I close my eyes and allow my mind to wander to the image of her in nothing but my shirt. My hand slides under the waistband of my sweats. It glides over the hard surface before I grip the base and slowly pull upward.

Fuck. It's been too long since I've had a release. With Leni always here I've gotten good at taking freezing cold showers. I come embarrassingly fast with the vision of her in my bed playing on repeat in my mind.

I lie panting in bed for a few more minutes before deciding to head out for a quick three-mile run followed by a shower. By nine-thirty I'm dressed and ready to head out to meet Leni.

I arrive ten minutes early for breakfast. Even off-season, this place is always packed. It's a sort of place that both tourists and locals can agree is worth the wait. It only takes me about five minutes to get us a table. I go ahead and order a coffee and water for both of us as well as a basket full of biscuits.

Right on time, Leni walks through the door looking beautiful but exhausted. She's still wearing the leggings and fall-themed sweatshirt she had on when we both left the house yesterday morning. Even still she blows all the other women in here completely away.

"Morning." She sits and starts mixing in some cream and sugar into the coffee the waiter just put down on the table.

"How was the night?"

"Long, but Nan rested a lot, so that's good. They gave her something to help her sleep through the night." She takes a bite of one of the biscuits and continues to talk with her hand blocking her mouth. "But I think I maybe got four hours total."

"Yikes," I respond.

"Yeah, but good news in that she's heading to the rehab facility today. I told them I'd be back in a couple of hours to help her move over there."

"That's great. I can help too," I offer up just as Lenny, the waiter, comes to take our orders.

While we wait for the food, I catch Leni up on the happenings at the station and she tells me about the slew of volunteers she's had in the library since Helen's hospitalization.

By the time the food arrives I'm starving. I'm used to eating around seven in the morning and it's now pushing ten-thirty. Leni must be hungry too because she eats her grits and eggs in the blink of an eye.

"Hungry?" I can't help but ask with a smirk crossing my face as she steals a couple of slices of bacon off the plate I ordered.

"Food was crap last night. Sorry, I should've ordered more."

"Have at it. I can always get more if I'm still hungry."

That's all the permission she needs to grab the two remaining strips off my plate. An hour later we've both gone back to her house.

She spends a bit gathering up everything Helen could ever need while I watch in astonishment.

"Does she knit?" I ask from my spot on the couch in complete confusion while Leni shoves a ton of yarn into a tote bag that reads 'Books are better than boys!' on the outside of it.

Never in all the time I've spent with them have I seen Helen knit or really do any sort of craft that takes concentration. Her attention span isn't long enough for that, not to mention her busy social calendar.

"No, well, she doesn't, but a few years ago she watched some videos online of people knitting obscene things and she thought it was hilarious. She bought all this planning on making it for her girls for Christmas."

"Okay," I slowly mutter, still not getting why she's packing it. "Did she ever make any?"

"Well, not technically."

"What does not technically even mean?" I ask through my laughter.

"Umm . . . she started one and got frustrated after an hour, so she went online and found someone who was selling them and bought a bunch for gifts."

Standing, I walk over to where Leni is now searching frantically through a packed cabinet. I grab her by the hand and turn her until she's wrapped in my arms. Without any prompting she wraps her arms around my waist and lays her head on my chest.

"She's doing better. She's going to be fine." I attempt to comfort her, knowing that her hectic energy right now is from worry.

Since her mom passed, she's struggled with dealing with change. She almost didn't leave to go to college to finish her degree because the idea of moving away terrified her. The entire time she was gone she saw a counselor at school.

She's gotten better over the years, but times like these I see her regress. It tears me up inside watching her struggle. I'm supposed to be able to take it all away, but I don't know how to fix this.

My shirt is dampening from the silent tears that are falling from her eyes. I just hold her and let her get it out. Once her tears have all dried up, I place a kiss on the top of her head and pull back to look her in the eyes.

"Take a short nap. I'm going to pack a suitcase for her."

"I can't. You don't know what she needs. I gotta do this."

"You're exhausted. What you have to do is rest for an hour. I will pack up the necessities and grab her iPad. She's less than ten minutes away. I promise if anything is forgotten or she thinks of something she wants I will personally drive it over to her at any time of day."

"You have a job, you know." She's back to herself, giving me hell whenever she can.

"I know, but I also know any of the guys would be happy to help if I'm unavailable. Now go lie down and take a quick nap. We need to be back at the hospital in an hour and a half."

CHAPTER 16

Leni

"I HEAR HELEN IS FINALLY MOVED OVER TO THE CARE HOME for rehab," Parker says as I walk into her place.

"Yeah, we got her settled over there last week. She's already organizing their social calendar from what I hear. It's a good place since it's a mix of independent living and rehab patients."

"Nice, Mikaela's so happy she's out of the hospital. I wouldn't let her go visit until she was released. Didn't want her in the way."

"I should be surprised news has already gotten to you that she's out but honestly in this town I'm not," I say with a chuckle.

"She and Mikaela have been texting for days." She pours us each a large cup of coffee and I've never been more thankful for anything in my whole life. "One day that girl's gonna need to make some friends her age, but I think it's great how close they are becoming."

"I can't blame her, though, Nan's pretty awesome. I was lucky to have her raise me."

"No wonder you're so kick-ass. Speaking of being kick-ass. Saw you coming and going from sexy McFirefighter's place. You finally jump that hot piece of meat? He's got muscles for days and eyes just for you."

A heat fills my cheeks and I can tell they are turning a bright pink. I stare straight down into my coffee cup, not wanting to make eye contact.

"Nothing scandalous, it's just been easier staying there than being in my place all alone."

"Hmm . . ." she says, seemingly unconvinced. "It's time for us to move into the next stage in this friendship."

"Umm . . ." I stutter. "Not sure I know what that is. Sleepovers? Karaoke? Face masks?"

"Nope. Though seriously when was the last time you had a girl-friend? Eighth grade?"

"No, of course not." I grab a pillow from beside me on the couch and cuddle with it in my lap. "I've never really had any girlfriends."

"Ahh." Pity fills her voice. "I get it. I haven't had a ton but then again, we moved around a lot my whole life."

I'm not sure why, but I feel a bit ashamed that I've ever really only been friends with Griffin and Nan. I never really desired any before but lately, with all the feelings and dreams I've been having about Griffin, it's been nice to have another girl to talk to.

"But for real, spill, girl. There's more there than what you're telling me."

God, I want to say it. I've never once said out loud how I feel for him. I'm too scared that if I say it I'll have to acknowledge how I desperately want more. It's just easier to bury it deep down and live it out in my dreams every night.

"I swear anything you tell me stays between us. Here, I'll open up first. I haven't had sex in two freaking years. Seriously, I am so desperate for dick it's embarrassing."

"You know you could have any man you want. You are textbook gorgeous."

"And I come with tons of debt and an eight-year-old girl who isn't mine. Now stop changing the subject. Spill the beans. Have y'all ever even kissed?"

"Me and Griffin? No, never. We're just friends. He could have any girl he wants. You should see them hang on him at the bar."

"Maybe. But from what I've seen that boy doesn't even give any girl who isn't you a second glance. For a smart chick you're a bit dumb, you know that?"

"Hey now," I say, attempting to hold my laughter in. I toss the pillow that's in my lap across the small room, hitting her in the stomach. Grabbing it after it falls on the floor, she sits down in the recliner chair, putting the pillow behind her head.

"I say that in the most loving, caring way possible. But the two of you are adorbs together. I'm a bit of a nosy bitch. I see how y'all take care of each other, not to mention all that Helen's told me."

"Gossiping turd," I whisper under my breath, causing Parker to let out a giggle. Apparently, I wasn't quiet enough. "That woman knows nothing, she just wants great-grandkids to corrupt one day. Pretty sure she thinks he's her only hope, seeing as how I never go anywhere without him."

"She ain't wrong," Parker says with her coffee cup in front of her mouth before she takes a giant gulp. "Now spill, how do you really feel about him?"

I stare down into my coffee cup, silent. This shouldn't be so hard to say, and I definitely shouldn't feel like I'm gonna cry at the thought of admitting it out loud.

"I love him. Always have. At night I dream he's mine to keep," I admit in one breath before throwing my hands over my mouth. I can't believe I just admitted all of that.

"Girl!" she exclaims excitedly. "Why on earth haven't you acted on it before?"

"I can't." I try as hard as I can to hold my tears at bay. "If I did and then lost him, or things went south, I'd be alone. He's my best friend. When my mom died, I was young, barely a teenager, and he was there for me. He's been by my side since."

"But don't you think the two of you deserve more? He wants you. I swear he does. I can tell these things."

"I dunno, I've always just been his goofy friend. Almost like a sister to him. The girls he's dated in the past, they were gorgeous. Like model pretty."

"Okay. I see we have a lot to unpack here. It's gonna require more than coffee. One glass of wine." She stands, grabs our cups, and walks across the room into the adjoining kitchen, opening the fridge and pulling an unopened bottle of wine out.

"I'm not a big drinker, but after these past few weeks, I think I'll take a glass. I could use it," I say, following behind her, surprising myself with my eagerness.

"No doubt, girl, now drink this while I lay it out there for you." She hands me a plastic cup covered in cartoon fruit with emoji faces on them. Smiling, I take a big sip of very sweet wine. Thank God for North Carolina muscadine wine.

We both walk back to our seats in the living room, cups in hand.

"So, here's what I think, you ready?"

"I dunno but go ahead." I take another sip, trying to mentally prepare myself for what's coming.

"That boy loves you," she states flatly as if it's fact.

"I know he loves me," I interrupt, setting my cup down on the table.

"Let me finish. That boy loves you, but in an 'I want to see you naked every morning in my bed' sort of way. I see how he looks at you when you aren't paying attention." She chugs her cup and walks into the kitchen for a refill. A second later she's back with a full cup and the bottle too.

"Damn! Have you got some binoculars or something?" I spurt out accidentally.

"Told you I love some good gossip. Now when he watches you walk away, that boy ain't looking straight ahead. He looks you up and down with that head tilted to the side sort of way you do when you are attracted to someone."

"You're making that up." I can't let her words confuse me. I'm not the girl for him.

"Hush, I'm telling you the truth. Now you go on home tonight and tell me you don't start to see the signs. The small ways he flirts. He wants you as much as you want him, and you are both dumb as shit."

"Rude," I joke, knowing she's just being silly.

"I really like you, Leni, I just want you to be happy and if he thinks you aren't interested, he will never make a move. He thinks you're fragile and easily hurt. He ain't gonna do it. You are going to have to make a move."

"How much do you talk to my grandmother?" I ask, finishing off my cup.

"Enough."

It's been three days since hanging out with Parker. Everything we talked about has been weighing on my mind from the moment I left her place. Nothing feels the same anymore. I spent yesterday hanging with Nan and her new friends over at the home and I couldn't get out of my head the whole night.

Griffin was on a three-day, two-night shift at the station, something he doesn't do very often, and I have only seen him for lunch once. Tonight's the first night he's been home since I talked with Parker and I can't decide what to do.

Now that I've admitted my feelings out loud, I don't want to take it back, but messing up our friendship isn't worth any risk. I can't lose him.

I pull into my driveway after work and immediately walk across the lawn to the place I keep accidentally calling home. But it's fake. I don't live here and eventually, I'll have to go back to Nan's place or worse yet move to my own place and be even farther away from him. The thought of not being right next to him is terrifying.

Griffin's truck is already in his driveway and I'm happy to see him back here. I've missed him at night. It's hard being alone and I don't like it. Everything is just better and more fun when he's near.

"Honey, I'm home," I call out as I walk through the front door.

"Hey, I made dinner," he tells me as he walks over and gives me a kiss on the forehead. Something he's done a million times over the years.

It's innocent and yet shivers run through my body. I get a good look at him and burst into full-blown laughter.

He's wearing his dark jeans that fit him perfectly, a tight gray T-shirt, and over the top of both is my beautiful floral apron with a gingham ruffle all the way from the top by his chest and around the whole apron. He's adorable and hot.

Just as I'm about to give him a hug hello, I feel a familiar sweet face at my ankles.

"Meow," Toby calls to me from the floor where he's weaving in and out of my legs, rubbing them in a desperate plea for attention.

"You got Toby!" I shout with excitement as I bend down to pick him up. It's not like I haven't seen him in the short time since I started staying over here. I've gone by the house during the day to get what I need and pet him some and make sure he has food, water, and fresh litter.

But since I can't seem to bring myself to go in there at night since it reminds me of finding her lying on the floor he's been there alone at night.

"Yeah, well, I figured with you here it was only right. Plus, I've missed the little guy. Should've done it sooner. Dinner's almost done. Why don't you go freshen up and I'll set the table."

"You didn't have to do all this. I feel bad, I'm already all in your space. I should be the one taking care of you while I'm here."

He sets the spoon he was stirring down next to the stove and turns the burner to low before turning and walking over to where I'm standing in the entryway.

"Leni," he starts, his voice calm, as he places his hands on my cheeks. "Don't ever think that I don't want you here. You belong here and knowing you'd be around had me excited all day."

I take a deep breath and nod. Once he goes back into the kitchen, I head to the bathroom to splash some water on my face. A lot is on my mind this week after talking with Parker. I feel his presence in the doorway before I even see him. He's always done that to me. I just instinctively know when he's around. A sense of comfort fills me whenever he's near.

"You about ready to eat?" he calls out from the kitchen.

"Yup, just cleaning up a bit." I look up ahead only to see him staring at me in the mirror. Our eyes connect for a moment and both of us are silent. Absentmindedly, I let my tongue lick the outside of my lips while our eyes connect in the mirror. I swear in that one second my heart skips a beat.

Overwhelmed with emotion, I do the one thing I promised myself I'd never do.

I throw the towel onto the floor. I turn and hastily take the three steps over to him and with a passion brewing deep in my soul, one I never thought would bubble to the surface, I kiss him.

It's innocent and just on top of the lips. He's frozen beneath my lips and regret fills me. I've ruined us. I pull back and try to get past him in the doorway. Ready to run. I need to get anywhere that isn't here. Oh, God. What did I do?

"Oh, no you don't." He barely gets the words out of his mouth before he's on me. I'm up against the wall. Silently staring up at his face. There's a look in his eyes I've never seen before.

Desire.

CHAPTER 17

Griffin

MY LIPS ARE ON HERS BEFORE SHE CAN SAY ANOTHER word. Leni Hughes just made every dirty thought I've had become reality in two seconds, and I have no intention of letting her run away from me right now.

Wasting no time, I use the tip of my tongue to beg for entry. I lick the line of her lips. My eyes close, terrified she's going to stop this. I've waited too many years for this moment, and it can't already be over.

A second later I feel her lips break open and I waste no time. My tongue glides in and tangles with hers. It's passion and fury and better than any wet dream I ever had as a horny teenager lusting over the girl next door.

We're already close, but I need to feel more of her. I'm desperate for her touch. I need to feel her up against my body, her hands tangled in my hair. I need it all.

"Not ready for reality," I pant out. "Need more of your mouth." I expect her to fight, but instead, she lets me lean into her and we're back to making out, standing against the wall in my master bathroom. I'm harder than I've ever been and all I want to do is push in closer so she can feel what she does to me. I don't know if she's ready for that yet.

Her hands wrap around my waist and pull me into her. Fuck yeah. The minute my cock comes into contact with her body she tenses, and

I expect her to pull back, but instead, it seems to egg her on. She's full of intense passion and I don't have any intention of stopping until she's ready. I have no clue how long we're kissing, but we're both panting when we pull away.

"This isn't right," she says breathlessly, pulling back away from me. "We need to stop. This isn't what we do." No. We're not undoing this. I can't lose this; I've been waiting forever for any sign that she has any sort of romantic feelings for me and now that I know she's attracted to me I can't lose it.

"Yeah," I respond, wiping the sweat off my brow, all the while still holding on to her waist. I run my fingers up and down her sides, feeling her shiver under my touch. "But . . . what if it was?"

I lean in again and place a slow, patient kiss on her swollen lips. The kiss we just experienced was passion and full of urgency. The sort of rushed decision that took us both by surprise. But this one is nothing but intention and forethought. She needs to understand how much I want this.

"Breathe, Leni," I whisper to her as I pull back just a few inches. "Stop overthinking this."

"How can I not overthink this? We just kissed." Her face is flushed with passion, but her eyes tell another story, one full of worry and doubt.

"Have you ever thought about this before today?" She motions, her hand pointing from me to her and back. "Have you ever considered what it would be like if we were more than friends?"

"Of course," I don't hesitate to reply. "I could say I've thought about it daily since puberty. Well, that might be a lie." I see her face fall, but I don't give her time to start lecturing me about being honest. "It's probably more like hourly."

Her eyes widen and I see a spark of interest flash through her eyes before she quickly conceals her true feelings and lets doubt take over.

"But you're my best friend. The only constant in my life besides Nan. And now more than ever I'm worried about losing you too."

"You could never lose me, Lens. But I've been dreaming about what your lips would taste like since I first noticed your strawberry Chapstick. Between that and your peach shampoo, I get half hard walking through the fruit aisle at the store now."

Desire floods her eyes and her lips part enough for her tongue to lick the top of her lips. When she doesn't pull back from my touch, a small growl escapes my throat. I use our current position to pull my body tighter into hers as her tongue explores my mouth.

"I know romance novels aren't real life. But this kiss feels epic and dreamlike. I'm scared, Griffin. What if it's a dream?"

"This is our life, Lens, let's have dinner and I'll prove to you that I can be your best friend and more all at the same time. Just don't run from this. Give us a chance to figure this out." I refuse to let her down. I'll prove to us we can have it all.

She grabs my hand, giving it a squeeze. Not letting go, I lead her to the kitchen table where our food has gotten cold and set her down. I grab the plates and reheat them and we eat, catching up on our day. It feels normal and yet every time our eyes meet, I see a twinkle of excitement in hers that I know is met in mine.

By the time we make it to bed after dinner, we're both exhausted from work and the emotions of the day, and after several chaste kisses with her small giggles escaping in between we both pass out with my arms wrapped around her and her hands holding mine tight through the night.

I wake the next morning alone, other than Toby scratching at my feet, begging for attention. I slept harder than I have in a long time. A quick glance at the clock tells me it's already ten in the morning. Leni is long gone to work.

I decide to get up and go for a short run before showering and having some breakfast and coffee. It's November here and it's getting cold. The winds from the ocean make the air extra harsh, but I wouldn't trade it for anything.

I find myself running through the town and as I'm passing the library, I see Leni talking to Ian outside. Instinctively my blood starts to boil, but I remind myself that she's just a friendly person. He probably ran into her on the sidewalk; the station is just a few doors down.

I should stop staring and finish my run, but I can't. I just keep watching as her face sours and she hastily turns and heads back into the library. With a smirk on his face, Ian walks in the direction of the station.

As if on autopilot I cross the street and head into the library. Leni is behind the counter scanning in books and organizing them on her cart.

"Hey, Leni," I call out as I enter the small library.

"Oh, hi," she says nervously. "I didn't expect you this morning. Isn't it your day off? I thought you'd be asleep until I got off work."

"Was just out for a run and thought I'd stop by before heading back." I wait to see if she's going to offer up what upset her.

"Good run?" she asks while gaining her composure.

"Yeah." I'm confused. She never keeps anything from me, but she was clearly upset before. "Was that Ian I saw outside?"

"Oh." She pauses. "Ran into him on the street. He could talk all day, and I had to let him know I had work to do."

It's believable and she never lies, so I'll let it go, but something still feels off.

"Okay, I missed seeing you this morning," I say, changing the subject, not wanting her to be upset. I make a mental note to keep an eye on Ian. He's always rubbed me the wrong way.

"You looked too cute sleeping, bit of drool on your pillow. You've been working so hard lately I didn't want to wake you."

"Wake me next time," I respond with a wink. "I don't want to miss any chance I have to kiss you goodbye." I lean in and place a chaste kiss on her lips. She blushes as she looks around to make sure no one saw before smiling and giving me one more sweet kiss on the lips.

"I'm going by to see Nan after work tonight," she tells me. "I'll be a bit late."

"Okay, I'll heat us up some leftovers. Wanna watch that new serial killer documentary on Netflix tonight?"

"Sounds like a plan." Her smile is genuine and she's back to being my Leni. I lean over the counter to kiss her forehead, knowing she's at work and this isn't the time to talk about last night. "I'll see you at home tonight."

Several hours pass with me doing my normal day off stuff, cleaning, house projects, and such. I've always been a clean and organized person, but since she started staying here I feel even more compelled to show her how smoothly this can go.

I'm just about to lie down and catch up on some TV when I hear my cell ring. I'm not surprised to see it's my dad. We talk several times a week. He's still to this day one of my favorite people in the world.

"Hey, Dad," I answer the ringing phone, happy to talk to him. We've always been super close. Heck, he's the reason I joined the fire department.

"How's it going back home?" His perpetually cheery voice brings a smile to my face.

"It's going, work is good." It's the slow time of the year, so we've been busy with new training and upgrading some equipment.

"How's Helen doing? Mom and I have been worried about her since we heard about the incident."

"She's doing better every day. She's gonna be in rehab for a bit, but the doctors are expecting a good recovery."

"That's great to hear. Your brother is coming to town for work and thought it'd be fun to visit. You cool if he crashes at the house?"

My brother, Shane, and I aren't exactly close. He's a couple of years older than me and while we've never had anything drastically bad happen or any major falling out or anything, we just grew apart as we got older. But he's family and family is family.

"Of course he can, why didn't he just call me, though?"

I know the answer. He knows I won't say no to Dad. But what a bit of a shit to assume I'd say no to him either.

"You know Shane, he's so busy with work. They have him working a million hours at the firm."

"Mr. Bigshot," I mumble under my breath. Shane has an air about him, that he's better than the rest of us townies because he went to college and didn't get a 'blue-collar' job. I know he doesn't mean to come off as arrogant, but he always does.

"This will be a good chance for the two of you to reconnect," he tells me.

My parents insist I'm reading too much into everything and they are probably right.

"Yeah, I'll try," I assure him.

I hear Dad grumble something about grown-ass men, but I don't acknowledge it. I know he's right.

"So, when's he coming to town?"

"In a couple of weeks. He's staying there for a few days then heading back to Raleigh."

"Okay, great." I attempt not to sound annoyed. "I'll get the spare room ready for him. I'll text him to make sure he still has his key in case I'm working late when he gets here."

I don't tell him about Leni staying at my place every night, or whatever else this is that we're doing. We haven't had any official talk and I don't know what she's wanting right now. We need to figure out what this is just the two of us before we start telling others.

The next two weeks have passed by in the blink of an eye. I swear you would think we've been living together for years based on how in sync we seem to be. With Helen improving every day at the rehab, Leni has gone back to the library full-time. Our schedules don't always match up, but even when they are opposite, we find a way to see each other every day.

CHAPTER 18

Leni

"I BROUGHT YOU A PLANT." I WALK INTO NAN'S ROOM, holding the too big fern I've named Bertha.

"Why in heaven's name would you do that?" she states from her bed where she's lying waiting for the physical therapist to come help her up. "Aren't there enough things dying around here?"

She's finally healing and working on her movement. I'm so proud of her for working so hard to get back to being independent.

"To liven up the place," I say with a smile, setting the fern on the table next to the one window in the room.

"If you wanted to liven up the place you should have brought some eligible bachelors with working hips and knees."

"Nan!" I cry out in surprise, not that I should be, she's always been a bit too forward. It's something my shy self just had to get used to. "Anyway, this place is so dreary, and I saw this baby at the store when I was getting you stocked up on magazines and snacks and decided you needed her in here." I look around at the stale gray walls and fluorescent lighting. "Plus, it really can't get worse." I take a seat in the chair next to her bed, thankful she was able to get a single room.

"Well, thank you. What's new? What's the gossip?"

I try my best to hold in the deep blush I know is attempting to form on my cheeks. I'm not ready to talk about me and Griffin, but I won't lie if she flat out asks me.

"Been hanging out some with Parker. I like her," I tell her, hoping that holds her over. I usually tell her everything, but I want to keep what's going on with Griffin and me to myself just a bit longer until we decide where we are going from here.

"I like her too, and that Mikaela is a spitfire. Reminds me of me when I was young."

"She's something special," I agree. "I know she's missing having you around. Any clue how long you'll be in here?"

"Is she the one eager to get me home or are you and Toby lonely?"

"Well, of course I miss you. Not sure about Toby, though, but actually, I haven't been staying at the house the past few weeks," I admit, unable to not tell her the truth. Sometimes my honesty is my best feature and sometimes it's my worst.

"You haven't?" She sits upright at the thought of gossip. If anything in the world could give her the energy to get out of her bed, it's the promise of good gossip.

"No, it was just too quiet in the house. Never realized how loud you were and how used to that I am." I grab a magazine off the table and use it to cover my face, knowing if she gets a good look at me she'll know everything I've done.

"Oh, really." I see her smirk from over the top of the magazine. "So where exactly have you been staying? With Parker?"

She thinks she's clever. She knows if I was staying with Parker and Mikaela then I would have told her about it.

"No, I've been crashing with Griffin. He offered the night you went into the hospital." I'm flipping through the magazine I brought her, not paying attention. I can't look up at her right now. "Didn't feel right staying at our place without you."

"Hot damn! Finally!" she yells out. Actually yells. I'm half expecting a nurse to come running in to check if everything is okay in here. They are probably so used to her antics by now that this isn't surprising.

"What do you mean finally?"

"Finally, the two of you are not tiptoeing around the fact that you both love each other," she states, a knowing grin on her face.

"Of course I love Griffin, he's my best friend." I put the magazine down and grab my phone that's buzzing in my bag.

"Bullshit, Peaches, you love him in a 'want to have all his babies' sort of way."

"It's not like that," I say quietly, hoping I can convince myself it's true.

"Sweet girl, it's okay to be scared, but please stop letting it control you."

I sink into the faux leather chair next to the bed.

"But in the spirit of enjoying your visit, I'll stop harping on you and change the topic. Did I tell you Leonard visited me yesterday?"

"Mr. Perkins? Why on earth would he do that?" Instantly I realize how mean that sounds. "Not that anyone wouldn't want to come see you, but he's so grumpy. I didn't even realize y'all were friends."

"He's not that bad. He's just not good at expressing what he wants. He brought me those flowers from his garden." She points to the most beautiful bouquet on top of her dresser.

Not knowing how to respond I finally look down at my phone and check my missed message.

GRIFFIN: Dinner tonight?

I can't control the huge smile on my face when I see his name. He's always been my person, the one who just gets me. But now there's something more. A sense of anticipation whenever I see him.

ME: Duh! Don't we eat dinner every night?

GRIFFIN: I want to take you somewhere special.

ME: Oh, like a date?

GRIFFIN: Yes, it's time we do this right.

ME: I like that. Where are we going?

GRIFFIN: It's a surprise. I'll meet you at home at six.

Home. The idea of me and him having a home together has me smiling from ear to ear. But I need to remind myself that this isn't permanent. I've got to leave at some point. I've been telling myself it's time. Nan's doing better and she's happy and I'm a full-grown adult who can stay in her house by herself.

I'm not as much scared anymore as desperate to keep waking up every morning next to Griffin. I love him holding onto me as if he never wants to let go. I love the sleepy look on his face before his morning coffee, and I love knowing it's only me who gets to experience these intimate moments.

But I don't have any clue how he's feeling about me being in his space all the time. He's been living alone for quite some time now and I just barged in and never left.

It's been forever since I've gone on any date, let alone one with the boy I've always loved. I want tonight to be special. I decide to call Parker on my way home to see if I can borrow an outfit. Other than the dress Nan bought me before the night out at the bar I only own sweet sundresses and outfits that are probably better suited for middle schoolers and elderly women.

"Hey, lady," she answers on the first ring.

"How's it going?" It's been a week or so since we've had the chance to talk and I honestly miss her company. I never envisioned myself with girlfriends, but I think she's a keeper.

"You know, just life. Keeping up with the hellion and trying to pay bills and all that jazz. How have you and Mr. Sexy Fireman been doing? Noticed you have almost exclusively been coming and going from his place lately."

"Umm . . ." I stutter, trying to think of a response that isn't giving too much away nor is it lying. "We've been good. Things with us are progressing."

"Please God, tell me you're banging that toned piece of pie."

"Pie?" I burst into laughter while avoiding the question.

"Hush, I'm tired and I've been working all day."

"We have a date. Our first date. Tonight," I say quietly into the phone.

"Yes!" she yells into the phone.

"You're awfully invested in something happening between me and Griffin."

"Girl's gotta live vicariously through someone and you're my only friend."

Crap, I've been a pretty shit friend lately. Between Nan and everything with Griffin and me, I've barely spent any time with her.

"Wanna go get coffee tomorrow? My treat."

"You know what, that would be great. Other than customers I've only talked to Mikaela lately and while she is always quite entertaining, it's not the same as hanging with another adult."

"Great, it's a date and speaking of dates I have a favor to ask."

"Sure thing, whatcha need?"

"An outfit that doesn't scream childlike or elderly."

"I got you, girl. Want me to meet you at your place or do you want to come by mine?"

"I can stop by yours if that's okay. So, you don't have to bring clothes over." Even though she knows I'm at Griffin's place most of the time I don't feel ready to fess up to basically living there right now, so I'm relieved that she's fine with me coming over to her place.

A bit later, I've checked in with Toby, gotten a snack, and I'm walking across the street to Parker's place.

"Word on the street is you have a hot date tonight," Mikaela says to me from where she's sitting on their front stoop as I head up the driveway.

"Who told you that?" I ask, sticking my tongue out in a playful manner, knowing full and well that she heard it from her aunt since no one else knows.

"Helen," she says flatly, stopping me in my tracks. No way I heard her correctly.

"You mean your aunt told you?" I check.

"Nope." She pops the P while she stands and walks back inside.

I'm hot on her heels. "That can't be right. I didn't tell her."

"She said she saw your text messages and was too excited and had to tell someone."

"She called you?" I stop in my tracks to look directly at her.

"Naw, I happened to call her right after you left, so I was the lucky girl who got to hear all about how you better not mess this up."

Great, by now the whole town probably knows. We aren't keeping it a secret, but having a bit more time to figure us out would be nice.

An hour later Parker's had me try every outfit in her closet. I'm putting on the last piece she set out. The one I've been putting off, hoping she would deem one of the other ones perfect before I got to it. But each time I put on a different, more conservative shirt or dress I know is not right she asks when I'm gonna put on the red dress.

Red is a color I've always avoided for fear that it would clash with my hair. Not to mention the fact that it's a color that screams look at me. I'm just not one for calling attention to myself. I prefer to fade in the background. But tonight, I want Griffin to look at me and deep down I know that this dress might do the trick. I just need to build up the confidence to actually put it on.

"Come on, girl!" Parker yells from the other side of the bathroom door. "We're waiting to see your hot ass in that dress."

I take a deep breath. This is it. I open the door and walk out into her bedroom.

"Wowza," Mikaela announces. "Who knew you were hot."

"Mikaela!" Parker shouts out. "Manners."

"What? I was just saying she looks good." With a shrug of her shoulders, she walks out of the room, leaving just me and her aunt.

"You do look hot, though. Red is your color," Parker states while grabbing me by the shoulders to turn me to look in the mirror. "He's gonna die tonight."

I feel my face drop and quickly try to correct it, but it's too late. It's obvious she noticed.

"Sorry, bad choice of words," she quickly says. "I just meant he's gonna be speechless and unable to keep his hands to himself."

I say nothing, but I can't hide the smile on my face just thinking about his hands on my body. Parker insists on helping me straighten my wavy hair and puts a small amount of makeup on me. Who knew winged liner, mascara, and some red lipstick could make me feel so sexy?

I arrive back home just ten minutes before six and put my stuff away. Moments later I hear the door open and my heart starts racing. This is ridiculous. I've gone to dinner and movies and everything else possible in the small town with him. But tonight is different, tonight I'm going as his date.

I walk out of the bedroom while looking down at myself, my hands running down the fitted ribbed fabric of the knit dress. Even though I never wear anything like this it still feels like me in here. The comfortable fabric and the fact that it goes down to just above my knees. It's sexy without being too much for me.

I finally look up and notice Griffin is just standing in the doorway staring at me. I freeze, not sure what to do. This is all new ground for us.

"You." He starts walking closer to me. "Are." Another step toward me. "A vision in red." He's standing toe-to-toe with me.

I'm about to respond when he takes my chin in his hand and lifts my face up while he leans his down. Our lips meet and it's heaven.

The kiss is quick and leaves me desperate for more, but Griffin pulls back, grabbing my hand.

"You ready?"

"I am. Where are we going?"

"It's a surprise. But it's a little bit of a drive. You good with that?"

"Good with spending time with you where you're trapped, and I can tell you all about this amazing book I've been reading. It's so good and I've been dying to talk to someone about it, but with Nan not around you get to be the one to hear about it."

"No complaints from me. Let's head out."

Forty minutes later I'm finishing up telling him about the dynamic ending to the crime thriller I just read. We pull into a parking lot of an older building I don't recognize.

"Where are we?"

"It's a new restaurant that opened here. It's called The Literary Table. This place used to be an old warehouse and they've turned it into a restaurant and store."

"I do love an old building."

"I know," he replies with a smirk and a wink as he gets out of the truck and walks around to open my door. I beat him to it and he puts his hand out to help me out of the high up truck. Thankfully I put on flats much to Parker's despair.

He entwines our fingers as we walk toward the door. I can't help but look down at them and smile.

"What sort of store is here?" I ask as we walk in.

He doesn't respond. There's no need to. As soon as we enter, I see books everywhere. Old ones lining the walls around the room. A dozen small tables are in the middle of the open room. Candles on each table and dim lighting set the mood. I've never been anywhere like this in my life.

"This is beautiful and romantic. It's perfect. Thank you."

CHAPTER 19

Griffin

I CAN'T STOP STARING AT LENI'S FACE AS SHE LOOKS AROUND THE shelves lining the front of the restaurant. We're waiting for our table to be ready even though I made a reservation. But she doesn't seem to mind the wait. She's just moving shelf to shelf, calling out all the books she's read or wants to read. I've never seen her so excited.

We get our table and order some food and wine. I'm usually a beer drinker, but when Leni said she wanted some with her dinner I decided to just get a bottle for the table. I'll just have a glass, but if she wants more it's there.

She finishes telling me about the book and I hang onto her every word. The way she describes a story makes you wish it wouldn't end. She's entrancing. I hold her hand on the table the entire time. It still feels unreal that this is us. That I get to touch her like she's mine to keep. These last few days have been the hardest I've had in a while. I want to spend every moment exploring her and us, but I have a responsibility to my job. But tonight is all about Leni.

Surprisingly she's finished her first glass of wine before the meal arrives. She isn't a big drinker. I've only ever seen her drink more than one or two drinks in a day a handful of times and the last time she did was when her grandmother abandoned her at the bar.

"Thank you," she tells the waiter as he refills her glass before making sure we have everything we need.

"This looks delicious," I tell her as soon as the waiter leaves. Thankfully even though the restaurant has an upscale appearance they specialize in Southern comfort food. My fried chicken comes with garlic mashed potatoes and Leni got her absolute favorite food, meatloaf along with some roasted Brussels sprouts.

"I swear you get that meal any time it's on the menu, even at a fancy restaurant." I can't help but pick on her.

"What can I say, I love it. Momma used to make it for me before she got ill. It always makes me feel happy and loved."

We take our time eating, even though we've been together every day since Nan got hurt. We still never seem to run out of things to talk about. We're in the middle of debating what's better TV shows or movies when she reaches over the table and grabs the drumstick on my plate and takes a bite out of it.

"Hey now," I jest.

"Hey, it's a date. I can get away with stealing your food. Can't be mad at me on our first date."

I laugh a little too hard and I notice a few heads turn to us. I don't care. Being with her makes anything else unimportant.

We finish our meal and decide to split an apple pie with vanilla ice cream on top. She takes one bite and lets out an intense moan that has my cock threatening to respond. I silently beg it to cooperate, but then she gets a small bit of ice cream on her lip and all I can think about is licking it away.

"You have a little bit on the top of your lip," I tell her so she'll wipe it away and I can stop thinking very naughty thoughts.

I try to remind myself that it's our first date and she's scared about us becoming more. I need to slow down, but inside I want to take her home and take her to bed to do more than just the innocent cuddling we've become accustomed to. But she's not ready for that.

I think I'm finally out of the woods, but then instead of using her napkin to wipe the spot away she swipes her tongue across her top lip and now my cock is doing more than just threatening to get hard.

"Leni," I grunt out. "You gotta stop."

"Huh?" She looks confused. She's completely oblivious to what she's doing to me. "What am I doing wrong?"

"Absolutely nothing," I tell her. "But if you don't stop acting like that pie is going to get you off, I'm going to end up coming in my pants right here in the middle of the restaurant."

She looks shocked, her freckled face turns bright pink, but her eyes give away the excitement my words incite in her.

"Oh," she eventually says. "Sorry."

"Don't be sorry for anything other than the fact that we are almost an hour away from home and I desperately want to pull that top down and finally see if your nipples are the rosy color I've always imagined them to be." I know I'm going a bit too far. But her excitement from my words makes me want to see where this goes.

"Griffin," she moans out in a hushed voice as she wiggles in her seat.

Once I've gotten myself to the point that I can stand without embarrassing myself I get the check and we go to head out but not before Leni buys a vintage copy of *Little Women*. It's not an original or anything, but it's at least fifty years old.

We drive home listening to music and occasionally talking about work and Nan. She doesn't bring up what I said in the restaurant and I don't say anything else about it.

Walking in the door to my place, the air is thick, but she's been yawning since we left the restaurant and when I finally have her, I plan on taking my time.

"Let's go lie down and watch a movie," I tell her to lighten the mood. She needs to know there is no pressure. This was our first real date and I want many, many more. I refuse to scare her off before we've had our chance.

She lets out a large breath of air. "Yeah, I like that plan."

I put on some sweats while she changes in the bathroom out of the red dress. I'm sad to see it go, but then she emerges, her face washed clean, wearing my station T-shirt, and the dress is long forgotten. Done up she looks like a supermodel, but this Leni is the gorgeous girl I love.

She lays her head on my chest just as the movie starts. "Thank you for tonight. It was better than I ever imagined."

"You've imagined our first date before?" I can't help but ask.

She lifts up on her elbows and turns her head to look me in the eyes. "Too many times."

"Yeah?" I ask with a huge grin on my face.

"Yeah," she whispers.

I lean up on my elbows to take her lips with mine. I kiss her deep, my tongue invading her mouth while we lie back down. I need her to see how much I want this. I pull back to look at her, but she doesn't let me look for long before she leans down to kiss me again.

We kiss for what feels like hours, neither of us wanting this to stop but neither of us taking it any farther. We kiss like we're trying to make up for lost time. For all the years we should have been doing this. We don't stop until neither of us can keep our eyes open any longer.

It's been three days since our date, and I've been working night shifts the last two nights and Leni works during the day and we haven't gotten to see each other except for short lunches. It's not near enough time and I miss her.

The library is closing, and I've snuck away to see her for a bit before she heads out for the night. I just need the chance to kiss her and hold her close for a few minutes.

The place seems empty, but I saw her car out front, so I head inside and glance around and see no one here. I check my watch and see it's past closing time, so I help her out and lock the door.

I hear her soft voice singing in between the shelves and head toward it. I've heard her sing before. Her voice is sweet and angelic, but she's always been shy about it. The closer I get the clearer the song is.

Her sass is coming through with each verse of "Shoop" by Salt-N-Pepa. I sit at the end of the row, listening to her as she gets more and more into the song. I peek through some books to see her sexy hips swaying as she shelves books.

Damn, she had to wear a little sundress. Even when the weather is cool she can't resist wearing them. I swear she does it just to torment me. She looks like a dream and I'm ready for a nap.

A small chuckle escapes and immediately she freezes. Not wanting to scare her, I turn the corner to the front of the aisle.

"You scared me!" she exclaims as her hand lightly smacks my chest.

"I couldn't help it, you were too cute." I put my arm around her and pull her into my chest. "I missed you today."

Rising up on her tiptoes, she places a loving kiss on my lips. As we kiss my hands take over and slide down her body, gently holding her waist right above her ass. I freeze, waiting for a reaction, not wanting to push her farther than she wants. This idea of us being in an actual relationship is still so new and I'm worried she's going to get scared and run. But she doesn't flee.

With that simple slide of my hands, I seem to have awoken a side of her I didn't even know existed. She clings closer to me and our kisses become more and more intense. I need to slow this down. We're in the library, it's her work, and it's a public place.

I should say something. I should pull back. But with her lips on mine and her hands creeping up under my T-shirt all rational thought has escaped. All I can think about is this girl I've been fantasizing about since I was a teenager.

The feel of her body flush with mine is better than anything I could have imagined. I'm in a haze of lust and I'm not sure how to slow down without her stopping this. Something she doesn't seem to be attempting to do.

"Griffin." A whisper of my name escapes her lips as I pull back to look at her. I can't hold back when she looks at me like that and before I can even react, she's on me. Her arms are pulling me in and my leg is quickly pushed between hers as her short sundress rides up her beautiful milky thigh.

"Sweetness," I moan between kisses. I'm trying not to rush anything. I want to live in the moment and enjoy the feel of her pushed up against me, but the feel of her straddling my leg with just a small piece of fabric separating her pussy from me is driving me insane.

She scooches a bit closer to me and I can tell the moment she feels my painfully hard dick. Her eyes widen and a look of utter desire courses through them. I'm so turned on it's taking every bit of willpower I have not to lay her across the checkout desk and bury my face in her hot pussy.

I settle for allowing my hands, which have been safely placed around her waist, to slowly move downward. I cup her ass and a moan escapes her mouth.

"We're in the library. We should stop," she says in the most non-convincing way possible.

"Is that what you want? Because if you do, I'll back away, but you need to tell me to stop because otherwise there isn't any way I'm quitting. You gotta tell me, baby," I ask as one of my hands delicately strolls past her thigh to where her cotton dress ends.

My eyes never leave hers as my hand finally makes contact with her skin. Her head shakes from side to side, letting me know that her willpower, much like mine, has vanished.

"You sure?" My hand is slowly creeping under the hem of the dress.

"Touch me, dammit," she demands, her voice gravelly and desperate. I thank God there are no windows nearby and that this place hasn't been updated since the seventies. With the door locked and the rows of books between us to hide us from view just in case, I do what I've wanted to do since I first hit puberty. My hand glides all the way up her thigh, taking in just how soft her skin really is.

I don't even notice I've been holding my breath until I feel the lacy edges of her panties. Once the lace and silk are under my fingers, I finally let out my breath.

"Fucking hell," I moan into her shoulder. "You're soaked."

"God, Griffin. Is this actually happening?" We're standing in the middle of the aisle, my body holding hers upright as her knees get weak.

"Fuck yeah, sweetness." I dip one finger under the lace. "This is happening. It's so long overdue. This was always going to happen."

I feel her wetness soaking my finger and all my patience flies out the window. Gently but with a sense of urgency, I push one finger into her tight pussy. Her head flies back and a low, deep moan surges out of her mouth. She's moving with me as my finger slides in and out. I add another and she's squeezing them, riding my hand, getting closer and closer to the finish line. I'm not ready for this to be over. I want to drag this out as long as I can in case this is a dream I'm about to wake from.

Reluctantly, I pull out and away from her. A whimper slips out of her mouth, but before she has time to protest, I turn her so her back is against the bookshelves and I drop to my knees.

"No, Griffin, you don't have to . . ." She doesn't have a chance to finish her sentence before I've pulled her panties down. She steps out of them with no further protest and I put them in my pants pocket.

Grabbing one ankle, I urge her leg up and place it on my shoulder. Without one drop of hesitation, I lean into her, my hand holding her dress up, and I take in the sight of her trimmed pussy gleaming, begging me to eat it up.

My tongue darts out as I lick her to the top. I take her clit into my mouth, gently sucking it. She immediately bucks and I let out a low chuckle. Knowing how desperate she is for me, I continue licking and sucking as she wiggles beneath my mouth. Her hands cover her mouth to keep her cries muffled.

She's getting close and I feel a sense of pride knowing that it's me getting her there. I pick up the pace, ready to drive her over the edge. Letting go of her mouth, her hands move to my head, tangling in my hair.

"More, sweetness?" I tease her, my tongue flicking over the outside of her.

"Dammit, Griffin, I'm so close."

"Tell me what you want." I've never been a dirty talker. I haven't dated a lot, but things have always been just the normal vanilla sort of sex life. But with Leni, I can't help myself. She drives me wild with her mix of innocence and desperation. "Say it."

A bright red flush covers her cheeks and the eye contact I'm always desperate for from her starts to break. But I'm not about to let her retreat away from this. I can tell what she wants. I can feel it on my fingers and taste it on my lips. She's eager and close and she wants it bad.

"Oh no, you don't," I tell her. "Look me in the eyes and tell me what you need."

"I can't say it."

"You can, baby, and you will."

"I want to come," she finally breathes out.

I place a loving kiss on the inside of her thigh right before I go back at her with my mouth and my fingers. It only takes a couple of minutes before she's pushed over the edge.

"Griffin," she calls my name out as the orgasm fully takes her.

As I stand up, holding her to my chest, we're both still breathing heavily. I wait until she's able to stand on her own before I let go.

"Umm," she stutters. "That was . . ."

"Delicious," I finish her sentence with a wink and her already pink cheeks darken. "How did I know you'd taste so sweet? Just like candy."

"Griffin." She slaps me in the chest. "You can't talk like that."

"You didn't seem to mind it a few minutes ago," I tease.

"That was different."

"I hate that I have to leave so soon, but I just stepped out of the station for a few minutes to see you. I gotta get back."

"Okay, you're going to be there all night?" she asks even though I'm confident she knows my schedule.

"Yeah, but I'll see you tomorrow." I tenderly rub the side of her cheek with my hand and then give her a kiss on the top of her head before I turn to head back to the station, hating that I have to leave her.

CHAPTER 20

Leni

I'M SITTING AT THE KITCHEN TABLE ENJOYING MY COFFEE BEFORE I have to leave for work when I hear Griffin's truck pull into the driveway. I'm not sure if I was hoping to see him or if I was hoping I'd miss him.

I'd be lying if I said I felt completely normal about yesterday. But I wouldn't change it for anything. I've wanted this for way too long to turn back now. I know at some point we need to talk about us and what all this exactly means. But for now I just want to be with him with no worries and no regrets. I take the last sip and put the cup in the sink just as the front door opens.

"Hey," I say shyly, looking anywhere but directly at him.

"Hey, yourself," he responds with a wide grin. If I had to guess I'd say he's not feeling awkward at all about what happened between us. "You weren't rushing to get out of here to avoid talking about yesterday, were you?"

"Would I do that?" I ask finally, to avoid having to own up to the fact that that is exactly what I was trying to do. I give up and look at him only to see him coming toward me with a gleam in his eye and a wicked grin on his face.

Instead of responding he gives me a gentle kiss. I don't know what I was expecting but having him still be the sweet man I've known for most of my life puts me a bit at ease.

"Go on now, I'll be here when you get back." He's still smiling like a damn fool and I just give him an evil glare.

"You know what? I'm looking forward to hanging with you tonight. I've missed you."

"I've missed you too, sweetness."

"The bed was lonely without you. Had to cuddle your pillow all night long." It's completely beyond my nature to just own up to what I want, but I'm in too deep. I need him like I need my next breath.

He kisses me deep and I start contemplating how bad it would be to open up late today but alas I know I can't do that. I step back and gather my stuff, heading out just as he goes to get ready to climb in his bed and get some rest for the day.

"You look different," Mikaela announces from her driveway across the street as I walk to my car on the way to work.

I look around and behind me to confirm she's talking to me. No way does this child know what happened or how sexy and alive it made me feel.

"Different how?" I cautiously ask.

"Hmm . . . not sure. But definitely different." With that she turns and walks back toward her house as if that was a perfectly normal thing to say. This girl astonishes me sometimes, but I do love having her around. She keeps things interesting for sure.

Shaking my head at the absurdity of this girl, I get in the car and head into work. Today is my favorite day, Children's Hour. I've put on my best Ms. Frizzle outfit complete with a skirt displaying the planets. Not something I would wear every day, but on Children's Hour days I can't help myself. I put my wavy hair up in a messy bun. Add a headband and go into the library.

By midday, the kids and their parents have all left and the small library is silent other than the occasional train passing by on the track behind the building.

I roll my cart through the rooms and in between the rows of bookshelves lining each section, putting away returns and generally just making sure everything is neat and tidy. With the building empty and me working alone I allow myself to listen to my favorite serial killer podcast, My Favorite Murder, through one earpiece. I'm so into the humor and crime that I almost don't realize when I get to the self-care section.

Looking around at the shelves I was pushed up against just yesterday, my heart starts to race and my cheeks flush. I spend a few too many minutes lost in my memories before I force myself back to reality.

I'm just regaining my composure after replaying the entire scene in my head when the bell on the door dings. Abandoning my cart and all my dirty thoughts, I start to head back to the front to greet the patron.

I'm half hoping it's Griffin here for a repeat or at least a small tease. I'm clearly becoming some sex-starved harlot in need of a good . . . I don't even get the chance to finish my thought when my eyes come across the one person in this entire town I dread seeing.

Ian Pharrell.

"Hello," I say through gritted teeth. There's no way in hell he's here to borrow a book. He's here to torment me. I'm not even sure if he really wants me or is just looking for a way to piss Griffin off. It's part of why I haven't mentioned anything to Griffin. If that's what Ian is after I'm not going to give him the satisfaction.

"Hi, beautiful," the smarmy bastard replies, taking a step closer. "You're fulfilling all my teacher fantasies in this outfit today."

Stepping back to keep my distance from him and his wandering hands, I make a mental note to burn the planets outfit.

"Eew," slips from my lips before I can hold it back. He's Griffin's coworker and I don't want to rock the boat for him, so I just try to keep my distance and stay away from the creep. But days like today when he actively seeks me out make me wonder if I'm doing the right thing. "What can I do for you today?"

"Well, isn't that a loaded question." His smile is as wicked as his words. How is this guy still working in public service? He's the worst of the worst.

"Are you looking for a book?" I try a more direct approach.

"Sure, got any Kama Sutra books?" Seriously, do lines like this work on any woman?

I swallow back down the small amount of vomit that came up and I tell him what section to go to. Five minutes later he returns with two books, one in each hand.

"Which one do you recommend?" he asks with an evil grin.

I walk around to the other side of the checkout desk, needing to put some safe distance between us.

"Do you have your library card with you?" I ignore his question and try to act as professional as possible. He comes in here at least once a week when he knows Griffin is busy and pulls some sort of stunt.

Ninety-nine percent of the time I love that I work so close to the fire station, but when he walks through my doors it's definitely the other one percent.

"I was thinking this one has more options for us," he says, flipping the pages, not acknowledging my question. "But the pictures in the other one are hotter."

A small gagging sound escapes my mouth and I attempt to cover it with a cough.

"Your card?" I repeat. "So I can check you out."

"You can check me out anytime you like, no need to ask." As if his words weren't bad enough, he adds in a wink and I have to hold down the vomit threatening to come up.

"Your library card, please," I clarify.

Before he can say anything else the walkie-talkie on his hip goes off, alerting him to a call. I shouldn't be relieved someone else is in distress, but being alone with him makes me so uneasy.

I spend the rest of the day distracting myself with work and planning new events to help encourage people to come in. By the time I get home, Griffin is already there.

Worn out, both physically and emotionally, I head in through the front door and fall onto the couch.

"Long day?" he asks, once again wearing his apron. I know he wears it to be funny and cute, but it does something to me.

"Better now that I'm with you." I stand to kiss him, still amazed that it's something I get to do whenever I want. Just for fun I follow him to the kitchen and wrap my arms around him from behind while he stirs the spaghetti sauce on the stove. One of the few meals he's perfected cooking that doesn't involve a grill.

I lay my head on his back and just hold on to him for several seconds. After he finishes stirring, he turns in my arms and leans down to look me in the face.

"You sure you're doing okay?"

"I am, I was just thinking today about how often it's you who's initiating our kisses and cuddling. I felt like holding on to you and even though I'm not a hundred percent sure what we are right now I followed my gut and came to you."

"What we are is a couple. You good with that?"

I think to myself with my head on his chest. "Are you sure we are going to survive this? What if something goes wrong? I'm scared, Griffin," I admit my worst fears out loud.

"I promise you no matter what you won't lose me. You can't ever get rid of me, I swear." He steps back so I can see his face. "If this"—he points between him and me—"doesn't work out we will still be friends."

"Promise?" I ask, still unsure.

"Promise," he says before leaning over and taking my mouth in a passionate kiss.

It's mid-week and I finally have a day off. After spending the day cleaning up next door, running some errands and helping Nan, I finally have time for a hot shower then I plan on spending the rest of my day on the couch with a book and maybe a little bit of Netflix.

"Hey, can you fill Toby's food bowl? I can hear him meowing from inside the bathroom." I yell out to Griffin as I wrap my robe on tight and start to brush my hair.

"Sure thing, baby," a voice that is most definitely not Griffin's yells back. It takes a minute for me to recognize it since I haven't seen the owner of the voice in what feels like years.

I burst out of the bathroom and run to the living room to give Shane a huge hug. Griffin mentioned a few weeks back that he might be coming by and possibly needing the couch for a night or two but since he didn't mention anything again, I figured it never played out.

"What are you doing here?" I ask as I hold my robe tightly closed around me.

"Work has me in Wilmington this week and I thought I'd just pocket the hotel money and hit up my brother since he has a perfectly good place right here," he explains. "Now what are you doing here?"

I try to hold in my blush, not that there's been much to blush about other than some late-night cuddles. But that's just Griffin being the sweet and supportive friend he always has been.

"It's been hard to stay at my place knowing Nan is in the rehab place. I've never been there without her. Griffin's been nice and letting me crash here."

"Oh, yeah," he says, a smile creeping up his lips. "Our boy is nothing if not sweet and kind, right?"

"Right," I mutter quietly.

"I guess that means you're in the guest bedroom?" His eyebrows rise in question.

"Sorry, did you need it? I can take the couch." I'm an awful human. Griffin and I just agreed this week that we're a couple and I'm already too much of a coward to admit it out loud. I'm breaking all my own personal policies just to not tell him.

"So you're in the guest bedroom, but you're showering in the master?" He's not buying anything I tell him.

"What is this? Twenty questions? It's a nicer shower." That is not a lie. Griffin upgraded the master bath last year and it is amazing. I could spend all day in there.

"I'll take the couch. I'm only here for a few days anyway."

"You sure? It's your brother's place. I hate to put you out."

"Naw, I'm good." He moves his small duffle from beside his feet over to the corner next to the couch. I'm an awful human. Why did I not just tell him the truth?

"Is that my big brother I hear?" Griffin walks in from the front door.

"Sorry, I was feeding y'all's cat. Whole neighborhood could hear her begging for dinner."

"Yes," I quickly interrupt. "Isn't he helpful? I was just explaining to him how I'm staying in the guest bedroom right now."

Griffin looks at me with disappointment but doesn't correct me.

"That's right. Hey, you want to stay over in her place? Might be better than the couch."

"Thanks, but I'm fine with the couch. I promise."

"Oh, yeah, well, I guess that means you're on the couch. It pulls out at least."

"No complaints here," he reassures us.

"I'm gonna go get dressed. I'll let you two catch up." I head down the hall to Griffin's room.

"Evangeline?" Shane calls out my full name, which he knows irks me. Only Nan gets away with using it.

I turn just as I get to the door. "Yeah?"

"Wrong room. Isn't that one"—he points to the room to the right of me—"yours?"

"Umm..." I try to stall while I think something up. "It is, but I . . ."

"She takes her clothes in with her usually when she showers so she doesn't have to walk around all exposed." Griffin has my back, like always.

"Yep, that's it. Gonna get dressed in the bathroom then we can figure out some dinner plans, sound good?"

"Sounds great. We'll be on the patio having a couple beers. Come on out when you're dressed."

I head into the master bath, locking the door behind me before I sink to the floor. I'm beyond frustrated with myself. Why didn't I just tell him that I'm with Griffin? This isn't like me.

I lied.

Me.

I honestly didn't even think I had it in me. Though technically I just didn't correct him. I just let him assume I was in the guest bedroom and I made no effort to fix it.

What is happening to me? I barely recognize myself. Standing, I quickly get dressed and gather as much of my stuff as I can in my arms. Peeking out through a small crack in the door, I make sure they aren't around, and I rush to the guest bedroom and toss my stuff on the bed.

I might not have corrected him before, but I will not lie now. I will be staying in here from now on. This is the best anyway. I was getting way too comfortable sleeping with his arms wrapped tightly around my waist to change that now. It can't last forever. I have to go home at some point.

I rush to make sure I'm acceptable before I join the boys outside. Over the years Griffin's told me how strained their relationship has gotten since Shane left town at eighteen. I walk out back to see the two of them sitting in the plastic chairs, each with a beer in hand and neither one talking.

"Calm down, boys, this party is getting out of control. We don't want the neighbors calling the cops on a noise complaint."

"Hilarious as always," Shane replies while Griffin just rolls his eyes. I know this isn't easy on him. He's always felt a bit inadequate next to his brother. Heaven knows why, he's obviously the superior Thorne boy.

"Shane," I say, grabbing a beer, trying to fit in, "tell us what you've been up to in the last few years. We haven't heard much from you since your parents left."

"Just working too much. When you're low on the totem pole in a law office you end up pulling a million hours a week. I have zero life to speak of."

"That's kind of sad," I say out loud accidentally.

"Hopefully, it'll be worth it in the end. But enough about me. Tell me about the two of you."

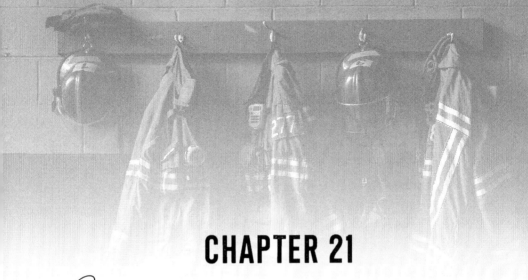

CHAPTER 21

Griffin

"Y OU WORKING TONIGHT? WAS THINKING WE COULD throw some steaks on the grill and have a few beers before you head back out of town," I ask Shane as he adjusts his tie and throws his jacket on. He's heading out for his meetings today and I promised Dad I'd try to spend some time with him while he's here.

When we were kids, we were the best of friends. We lived for days with Dad. The three of us spending the day together getting into trouble and having fun. But then he hit his teen years and he couldn't be bothered anymore. He kept flaking on our days and then he started acting like he wanted nothing to do with me at all.

At the time I took it personally. I was angry at him and stayed that way for too many years. Looking back, I get that being a few years older than me he hit his teen years and only cared about sports and girls and hanging with his little brother just didn't rank on his list of important things to do.

"Yeah, I'll be back around six. Dinner then?"

"Sounds like a plan. Leni's going to spend some time with Helen tonight, but she'll be back by later in the evening."

"Just an FYI, I'll be wanting some more details about what's happening with the two of you. I don't buy for one second that she's been staying in the guest room."

I don't respond, but the laughter that follows his statement is enough to tell me I'm not off the hook yet.

I spend the day working out, doing a few repairs on the house, and going to the store for some good quality steaks. By the time Shane walks through the door I'm already out back heating up the grill. It's an unseasonably warm night, a good reprieve from the cold winds we typically get this time of year.

"Hey, bro, I'm out back," I call through the open kitchen door. "Bring me a beer when you come out."

"Sure, just give me a minute to change out of this suit," he responds just before I hear the hall bathroom door close.

Five minutes later we're both sitting on the deck with a cold one in our hands, waiting for the steaks and potatoes to finish cooking. I love that Leni likes healthy food and makes sure we have greens at all our meals together, but there's something to be said about just having some good grilled steaks and baked potatoes.

"Why are you here?" I blurt out. It's been bothering me since he arrived. I didn't bring it up last night with Leni around, knowing it would make her uncomfortable, but he hasn't visited in years and I'm sure it's not the first time work has brought him in this direction.

"Honestly?" he asks, setting his beer down on the table.

"Yeah, of course," I answer, leaning back in my chair, ready to hear what he has to say.

"The last few years have sucked. I've worked my ass off in school, then busted my butt to get a good job. But I work a million hours and I can get lonely. Every time I talk to Mom and Dad, I have to hear about how amazing your life here is."

I'm shocked.

"What are you talking about? All they tell me is how proud of you they are. They go on and on about your life in the city and your new house, new car, and fancy job."

"Well, I get to hear about how close you are to Leni and Helen, all the times you save people's lives, not to mention the friendships you've developed at the station. Do you even realize how proud they are of you? I had to be in Wilmington, and I thought instead of staying in yet another cold, lonely hotel I'd come to see you and maybe some of your happiness would rub off on me."

"I didn't realize you were having a hard time. I just assumed your life was perfect."

"Far from it," he says through a laugh.

"Life's not perfect here," I tell him after taking another sip of my beer.

"Looks pretty perfect to me," he says. "You got the girl, the house, the job you always wanted."

He's not wrong, but he's also not a hundred percent right either.

"Yeah," I say, looking toward the house. "Still figuring out that first part."

"She might be denying it, but you can't convince me the two of you aren't together."

"We are," I say for the first time out loud to someone other than Leni. I haven't even told Jack yet and he's probably my closest guy friend. "But she's timid and not ready to tell anyone."

Now that the cat's out of the bag I open up and tell him everything, well, almost everything. We finish our beers just as the food is done. He grabs us another as I set the table. I never expected him coming here would bring us closer, but I'm actually glad he's here. We're both long overdue for a good conversation. We've let our differences as brothers define us for too long instead of allowing them to bring us closer.

Two hours later we're still sitting out back and we're each six beers deep.

I feel my buzz start to form. This is probably the best Shane and I have gotten along since we were kids. By the time I started hanging out with Leni he was already over spending his spare time with his younger brother. I remember being desperate for his attention and all he cared about was getting into college, getting out of this town, and getting all the girls on their knees.

To say we grew apart is an understatement. Somehow, even as we got older neither of us put in the time or effort to repair our relationship. I'm surprised how good a time I'm having with him here.

I get out of my chair to head inside to grab us each another beer. As soon as I turn around, I'm confronted with one of the worst things that could happen to me while I'm this tipsy.

"Shane!" I yell out as I notice the back door is wide open. "Shane!" This cannot be fucking happening.

"What?" he asks, walking back inside without a care in the world.

"Did you see Toby?"

"Toby?" he asks, a look of complete confusion on his face.

"The cat," I explain. "Leni's cat!"

"Oh, maybe he went out when I came in." He's not getting the gravity of the situation. I'm trained in remaining calm in tense situations and yet right now I am freaking the fuck out.

"Shit! Fuck! Shit," I say under my breath. I try not to get angry; it's not his fault. It's mine. I should have warned him.

"I'm guessing he's not an outdoor cat, is he?" He's running his hands through his dark hair, looking around.

"No, I should have said something. I'm not used to having a pet." I start to explain, sobering up. I can't have lost her cat. She will not handle this well.

"He can't have gotten too far. Let's look for him," he says, jumping into action.

I put the leftover food inside and we each take off in a different direction around the house.

Forty-five minutes later we meet back up defeated, neither of us having found Toby. I think I walked a mile calling out his name, even had a few neighbors out and about helping. Sinking down into the chair on the back patio, I try to work up the courage to call and tell Leni that Toby is missing.

"I'm going to hit the head and grab a beer. Want me to bring you one?" Shane announces as he stands.

"Yeah," I say, only half paying attention, my brain running a mile a minute trying to prepare myself for the conversation I'm about to have with Leni. She's having dinner with Nan at the rehab facility, but she will be home any minute.

"Hey, guess what I found in the bathroom?" Shane says from behind me as I will myself to hit call on Leni's number on my phone.

"Not now, I should call Leni and tell her I lost her cat."

"You might want to turn around before you make that call," he tells me, a hint of humor in his voice.

"What, Shane?" I say a bit too loud, annoyed he's making jokes right now. I know he's had a bunch of beers, but this is serious. I'm about to break the heart of the girl I love. She's not going to forgive me.

She's going to leave my house pissed off at how reckless I was. How can I expect her to open up to making a life with me when I can't even keep her cat alive and safe?

Reluctantly, I turn to tell Shane to piss off when I see the small gray cat curled up in his arms.

"You found him!" I jump out of my seat, relief flooding through my body.

"He must have gotten trapped in the bathroom the last time I was in there."

"Thank fuck," I say, rubbing Toby on the head. "Let's get him inside before he gets loose."

"Good idea," he agrees. "But we're taking a shot to celebrate."

"Shots, really?" I say, already pulling the whiskey from the cabinet.

Thirty minutes later we've had three shots each and Shane is now passed out on my couch. His legs are hanging off the end and he doesn't even have a pillow or blanket. But hey, at least he made it to the couch. It's getting late and I'm relieved to see Leni's headlights in the front window.

"Hi," I say quietly as she walks through the door. She looks at the couch at my brother, who's half falling off, fully dressed. Shot glasses are sitting on the coffee table and then she looks back at me.

"Y'all have a good night?"

"We did," I reply. "But I think I'm ready to go to bed."

"Oh, yeah? You tired?" she asks as she walks down the short hall toward my room with me on her heels.

"No, not even a little," I tell her as I shut the door and lean down to passionately kiss her hello. "But I missed you today."

"I missed you too." She leans her head to the side to give me access to her neck. A spot I'm quickly realizing is one of her favorites.

"Have I told you lately how incredibly sexy you are in these dresses?" I run my hand up her tights covered thigh. "Even with this underneath them, I can't help but think about you wearing them while riding my cock."

"Shh." She hushes me while looking through the doorway to where Shane is asleep on the couch. "You're drunk."

"Maybe a bit," I admit. "But that doesn't make it any less true." I kiss her and she doesn't hold back. She takes as much as I have to give. Our tongues are tangled together, and it feels like hours before either of us breaks free.

"Griffin," she pleads when my hands keep working their path up her thigh until I reach the apex of her legs. Even with her fully covered I can tell she's soaking wet for me.

"I got you, baby," I whisper in her ear as I gently rub circles around her most sensitive spots. She's wiggling beneath my touch, spurring me on, desperate to see her come apart for me.

She's close but before she gets to her breaking point she stands and pulls her leggings off. My eyes widen at her bold move.

"Your turn," she whispers, fully aware my brother is passed out on the couch just down the hall.

"Yeah?" I check with a tilt of my head. I might still be a bit tipsy, so I need to make sure I'm understanding what she's saying. "You ready? Now? With him out there?"

"I don't want to wait any longer. It's been hard enough being here with you not being able to see you and touch you completely."

I unsnap the button on my jeans, raising my eyebrows, making sure she has no regrets. But when I look at her, she's already pulling her dress over her head.

"Fuck me," I state in awe, looking at her in a matching pink lace bra and panty set. "What are you wearing?"

She looks down at herself before looking back at me.

"What do you mean? This is basically what I wear every day."

I close in the space between us. "You mean to tell me that every time I've had lunch with you at the library or hung out on the couch with you watching movies you were wearing sexy as fuck underwear under your cute outfits?"

"Yup," she says innocently while giving me a gentle push until I'm sitting back down on the end of my bed.

"Shit." I run my hand up her silky leg, playing out every fantasy I ever had of her standing over me in lingerie here in my bedroom. Putting my hands on the back of her thighs, I gently guide her toward me until she's straddling me.

I waste no time in taking her mouth. We kiss for what feels like hours and just when I think this can't get any hotter, she starts grinding on my dick, pushing us both close to a premature ending.

My pants are still on, just unbuttoned and she isn't having it. She pulls me to a standing position and without breaking eye contact she finishes unzipping my pants and pulls them and my boxer briefs down to my ankles.

I'm standing in front of Leni Hughes completely naked.

A small growl escapes my lips, watching her unhook her bra and letting it fall to the floor. Her small, perky breasts are begging for my mouth and I don't wait for her to make another move.

I drop to my knees and take one dusty pink nipple in my mouth. It hardens under my touch. Using my hand, I gently pinch the other one while I continue to lather my attention on the first.

"Griffin," she moans a bit too loudly.

I back up, letting her nipple pop out of my mouth. "Shh," I whisper, reminding her, using my head to motion toward the door. "Can you be quiet?"

"I dunno," she responds. "But I can try."

"I'm going to stop if you get loud," I tell her before I lean down and take her other nipple in my mouth. This time instead of using my other hand on her breast I use it to pull down her panties and throw them into the pile of clothes we've accumulated on the floor.

Before things get any further, I pull back. "I need to get a condom," I tell her.

"Um . . ." she stutters. "If you want." A pause. "I mean, I'm on the pill. You don't have to use one. That is, unless you want to. I understand if you do."

Holy. Fucking. Shit.

CHAPTER 22

Leni

E SITS DOWN ON THE EDGE OF THE BED, HIS TONED BODY and very large, very hard cock on full display. Fully clothed he is a sight to be seen, but Griffin Thorne in the nude is every erotic novel come to life.

He scoots back just a bit and grabs my hands to pull me onto the bed. Instinctively I straddle his body and for the first time my pussy makes contact with his bare cock.

I sit here for a minute just taking in the feel of him beneath me. Neither of us is talking. The room is silent except the sounds of our heavy breathing.

"If it already feels this good and I'm not inside of you yet, just imagine how good we're going to be together," his sexy deep voice whispers into my ear.

I hear myself gasp at his words. I need more of him but before I can allow myself to finally do what I've wanted for so long I look into his eyes in search of any sign of doubt. There's nothing there but desire and love.

Years ago, I'd resigned myself to staring at those lips forever and never trying for more. He's my best friend, my only real friend if I'm honest. But the way he's looking at me right now. God, he makes me want to risk it all just for this moment.

"We'll always be friends, right . . ." I don't even finish my question and his lips are on mine.

Lifting up slightly, I wrap my hand around him. I line us up and slowly and deliberately I lower myself onto the first several inches of his cock. I freeze, allowing myself a moment to take in the fact that he's inside me.

It's amazing. He's barely inside me and I'm already so full.

"Look at you on my cock," he says into my neck. "Knew you'd look amazing taking me in."

"Why do I love your dirty words so much?" I ask, lowering my body until he's all the way inside.

"Because it's me saying them," he says on a breath.

He's not wrong. I'm staring down at where we're joined.

"Is this real?" I ask, not looking up and also not moving. It's all so much.

"Feels real to me." His voice is strained. "But I'm gonna need you to move. Please, Leni, this is torture. It feels too good. You're too wet, too hot, too much of everything."

I don't stop looking to where we're connected as I lift my body and slide back down. My pace stays slow as I try to drag this out. I want to feel like this forever. Connected to him in every way possible.

But if the fingers digging into my ass are any indication, my slow pace is tormenting Griffin. Still, I slowly slide up his cock then plunge back down.

Suddenly, the hands on my ass lift me up and flip me over so my torso is on the bed but my feet are standing on the floor. I don't have time to mourn the loss of his cock before he plunges deep into me.

He relentlessly takes me while I muffle my moans into his comforter. It's too much. I'm so close and I'm trying to hold on so I can fall off that edge with him.

"Let go," he demands in my ear. "I'm right behind you."

I don't fight my orgasm. I let it roll through my body.

"Shit, you're squeezing me too good."

"Wow!" Is all I can say when his body finally rolls to the side of me. We're both drenched in sweat and breathing as if we ran a marathon.

I roll to stare up at the ceiling, holding in the giggle that's threatening to slip out. I just had sex with Griffin. My best friend Griffin.

"That was," he starts.

"Everything." I finish.

We both make our way to the top of the bed. Stroking my hair, he holds me sweetly and calmly until we both fall asleep, exhausted from the day and the activities of the night.

The next morning, I wake and he's still here, asleep beside me. His arm holding me tight to his chest.

A ding on his phone wakes him. He gives me the sweetest, kindest smile along with a gentle kiss to my lips before he rolls over on his side to check his phone.

Next thing I know he's burst out in laughter. I sit up confused, pulling the sheet with me.

"What?" I ask, curiosity taking over.

"Here," he says, passing me his phone, still laughing. "Read it."

I take the phone in my hand to read the text on the screen.

SHANE: Sounds like you had a better night than me. Got a call from my boss and they need me back in the office. When things settle down with the two of you, y'all should visit. I have thick walls so no worries.

I hand him back the phone, sinking back down onto the bed, pulling the sheet over my head.

"Come on," Griffin tells me, pulling the sheet down from over my head. "It's not that bad."

"Not that bad!" I say a bit too loud. "Your brother heard us having sex last night."

"But look on the bright side," he says, smiling from ear to ear.

"Bright side?" I exclaim as I pull the T-shirt he discarded on the floor last night up off the floor and put it on. "What could possibly be the bright side?"

"We had sex," he says, walking over to me in his full nude glory. "Does it get any better than that?"

I can't fight his logic, so I just slowly shake my head from side to side before he walks over to his dresser and pulls out a pair of dark gray sweatpants and pulls them on.

"Plus, I'm guessing next time Shane comes to town he'll get a hotel room."

Grabbing a pillow off the bed, I toss it at him, hitting him in the head.

"Hey now," he teases. "I will not apologize for fucking the woman I love."

I freeze.

"You love me?" My voice cracks as I get out the words.

"Of course I love you. Why do you think I bought my parents' house when they moved away?"

"I assumed they gave you a good price," I tell him in all honesty.

"I bought it because I couldn't stand the idea of waking up in the morning and not getting the chance to see you before anyone else. The idea of not seeing the sparkle in your eyes at night before I head back to my place after we binge-watch whatever show on Netflix you are currently stuck on."

My palms are clammy and my heart races. This is everything I've ever wanted and so much more.

"I love you too," I finally tell him the words I've been holding onto for too long. "I love you so much it hurts inside."

"Don't you know by now that you are the start and end of my days? You are my sunrise and my sunset." He's holding my face up, looking into my eyes. He's not letting me shrink away from this moment. "You mean everything to me."

Tears stream down my face. But hearing the words I've wanted to hear for so long come out of the mouth of the only man I could ever truly love has me so weak it's impossible to hold it all in.

"I got you a cupcake. Hope that's okay," Parker says as I sit down at the café table.

"Of course. Who doesn't love a little treat now and then?" I take a sip of the coffee I just got me. I need caffeine if I'm going to make it through the day. Ever since we first started having sex Griffin and I haven't been sleeping much.

"Well, if I can't have dick, I'm going to need chocolate," she says without stuttering. I love her blunt nature, but it's taken some getting used to.

I make the mistake of taking a sip of my coffee just as she started talking. I spit it out, laughing at the craziness that only she can come up with.

"Well, eat up," I say, taking another sip.

"Aren't you gonna have yours?" she asks, eyebrows raised.

"By your logic, I guess I should give you mine," I admit.

"You whore!" she says a bit too loud.

I sink down into my chair in embarrassment.

"Shh, before the whole town knows," I tell her. "Word spreads around here too fast. Old biddies are always listening and ready to gossip with anyone who's nearby."

"Fine, but details, now!" she demands while taking a large bite out of her cupcake. "Tell me that man's even better naked than he is in his uniform."

Immediately I start envisioning him all done up in his gear but then my mind wanders to the glorious sight I got to see. I snap myself out of my daydream.

"It was . . ." I stall, thinking of how to describe the best night of my life. "Amazing."

"Just amazing?" She raises her eyebrows up and down a few times, teasing me.

"Sorry, I warned you I'm not great at this girlfriends thing. It was the best night of my life. But that's all I'm saying right now." I pick up my cupcake and before she can pry any more, I take a huge bite out of it.

"Heard Helen is coming home this week," she says, changing the subject, thankfully.

"Yeah. I'm getting her after this actually. I'm excited. Probably more so than her."

"Really?" She leans back in her chair, confusion written on her face. "Aren't most people excited to get out of places like that?"

"Probably." I start to explain. "But she's so social and everyone there loves her. She's basically prom queen of the retirement community. There are friggin' clichés there now. If she stays much longer the men who golf will be ordering letterman jackets."

"I can see it. Mikaela's been heading over there after school most days. She's loving hanging with everyone. I didn't ask her to do that, but Helen insists she's a help to her and honestly it's been a huge weight off my shoulders."

"I'm glad Nan's taken her in. Even with going through a lot in my childhood, it was always still fun because I had her. She always finds joy in every situation and makes sure those around her do the same."

We finish our coffee. Parker needs to get to work for the night shift, so I give her a hug goodbye and gather up my jacket and purse.

I leave the café smiling from ear to ear. I never felt like I was missing out not having a lot of friends, but having Parker in my life has shown me I need more than just Griffin. Plus, I can't gossip about my relationship with Griffin to Griffin and while I'm comfortable talking about most things with Nan I draw the line at my sex life.

I just wish Nan followed the same code.

By the time I walk into Nan's room, she's already packed everything up.

"I was planning on helping you get your stuff together. I don't want you to hurt yourself," I explain as I start checking through drawers, making sure nothing's been forgotten.

"Calm down, Peaches. I'm not made of glass," she tells me, making her way over to the side of the room where I currently am.

"You're using a walker and under the care of a neurologist." I pick up Bertha the fern and set it over next to the door with the rest of her stuff.

"Sit down," she tells me, using her firm adult voice, the one she would break out in my teen years when I would avoid all responsibility for the sake of reading a good book. "We need to talk."

I don't fight her. I just sit on the bottom of the bed and wait for my lecture.

"I'm going to be okay. You are getting older, falling in love, you'll be moving out before you know it."

"I'm not . . ." I start.

"No interrupting." She gives me her best stare down and I just slump back into the bed.

"I will not allow you to waste your life scared of what could happen instead of enjoying the moment."

Tears threaten to fall, but I hold them in. "I don't know how to do that."

"You'll learn," she says. "But you gotta try. Promise me you'll try."

"I'll try."

"Good. Now I expect to hear more about your not so secret relationship with the boy next door on the way home."

CHAPTER 23

Griffin

THREE MONTHS HAVE PASSED SINCE LENI AND I STOPPED keeping our relationship hidden inside the walls of my house. For a week or two it was the hot gossip in town, though from what I can tell not one person was a bit surprised we'd gotten together. We've both been busy but still, we make time every day to see each other.

This is the happiest I've ever been in my life. I'm in my mid-twenties and I feel like my life is finally coming together.

Leni's been splitting her time between her place and mine, staying with Nan any night I have to work late, but if I'm in my bed before she's asleep she finds her way over here.

It's already the end of February and the weather is starting to look up. Today is my day off and for the first time in weeks Leni is off too. I have a special day planned, and like a kid on Christmas Eve the excitement is almost too much.

I wake up early, way earlier than her, I'm sure. She stayed at her place last night since I wasn't going to be home until late. I know I should sleep in. I've been working a lot of night shifts lately and it's starting to catch up with me, but I can't help myself. I have a whole day off with her and I plan on not wasting any of it.

I texted Helen last night to let her know I was coming over early so as not to scare her. I use my key and let myself in their place. It's already eight-thirty, but both of them are passed out. I start putting the supplies I brought on the counter.

I'm not even attempting to tiptoe around and yet neither wake. I make a mental note to talk to them about a security system. It's a tad concerning that I've come in and I'm preparing breakfast and neither has woken up.

Once I have the pancake batter mixed, I let myself into Leni's room. It's a sight with piles of books everywhere, not to mention the small Christmas tree she assembled by stacking her books in the shape of a tree and stringing lights around it in the corner. It's been two months since Christmas and I'm guessing it will be two more before she gets around to taking it down.

I almost burst into laughter at the sight of her sleeping. She's horizontal on the bed, Kindle hanging off one hand and her laptop on the bed open on the other side. The glow of the blinking lights gives her a glow about her. She's a mess but still looks like an angel.

"Morning," I say as smoothly as I can as I lower myself onto the bed next to her, careful not to knock anything over.

Sliding her laptop a safe distance away, I lie down beside her. After she wipes the drool from her lip and rubs the sleep from her eyes, she rolls to her side to look at me. Giving her a minute to fully wake up, I lazily run my fingers through her fiery hair and just stare at this remarkable woman.

"Hi," she says sleepily as she puts her arm around my side and pulls me in closer. "What time is it?"

"About nine," I tell her before I kiss her. "Happy Birthday. Now, why don't you get up and dressed? I'm making breakfast."

"Yeah?"

I scoot out of the bed. "Come on out when you're ready, we got a big day!"

Ten minutes later and the pancakes and bacon are done. Leni's sitting down at the table with a huge cup of steaming hot coffee in her hands. I give her a few minutes for the coffee to hit her bloodstream before I start talking. I'm a bit surprised that Helen is nowhere in sight, maybe she's giving us some space.

"Was Helen up late?" I ask while serving the breakfast. "Usually she shows up just in time to eat." Once we both have our plates full, I sit down at the old small table next to her. I'm starving and for someone who rarely cooks I have to admit this looks good.

"Pretty sure she didn't come home last night. Mr. Perkins picked her up for a date late yesterday," she explains between bites of food. She and Leonard have been steadily going out since she got home from re-hab. While still a bit of a grump the whole town is ready to throw her a parade for his overall improved demeanor. He rarely yells at the neighbors and isn't nit-picking everything everyone around him does. No one is quite sure why she's attracted to him, but no one wants to jinx it by questioning her.

"Is she healed enough for that much"—I take a bite to give myself enough time to think of a delicate way to phrase this—"activity?"

She completely misses what I'm saying or at least is ignoring the hint. Instead, she just replies, "Doctor says as long as she uses the walker when upright for too long, she's good to move around. She's even driving again, though he picked her up last night. She said something about bingo at the retirement center with their friends."

"Uh-huh." I decide against telling her that her grandmother probably stayed out late because she was getting laid. "I'm sure it just got too late to drive. She's joining us with Parker and Mikaela later tonight for cake."

"Yay!" she squeals. Leni's always loved her birthday and every year we have the same ice cream cake with Helen. She gets it from a local bakery and Leni waits all year for it.

"But before that, we have a fun day planned," I tell her while I clean up the dishes.

"Oh, really?" Joy fills her face. While not a big fan of big groups she's always enjoyed our adventures out just the two of us.

"Yup, but first things first, there's something I've been dying to do for the past few months and the timing has never worked out." I take a step closer to her and she takes a step backward. The predatory look in my eyes saying enough.

"What's that?" she teases. If the sly smile she's giving me tells me anything it's that she knows exactly what I want.

"You and me." I pause and see her eyes widen. "In your childhood bed." I take another step closer to her as she continues to back into her room.

A giggle escapes her mouth before she rushes over and jumps on the now clean bed.

"Well, then," she says, giving me her best attempt at a seductive look. "What are you waiting for?"

An hour later we're both sated, dressed, and ready to actually start the day. We head out, only running a few minutes behind schedule. It isn't until we've been on the road for thirty minutes that Leni finally asks where we are going.

"You really aren't going to tell me?" she asks, and I just shake my head in response.

It's just a few minutes later when we finally pull up to our destination and I see her eyes widen in excitement.

"What are we doing here?" she asks, looking around the marina confused. I lucked out and it's a pretty warm day for not even being the beginning of spring yet in North Carolina. With the weather here you really never know.

"We're going on a boat ride," I explain as I lead her through the parking lot and down a dock to what can only be called some sort of mini yacht.

"Really?" she asks, excitement filling her voice.

"We are." I let go of her hand and place mine on her back, guiding her up the ramp to where the captain of the boat is waiting to help her on.

One of the guys at the station's uncle owns this boat and called in a favor to help me make this a special day. I've spent many of her birthdays with her, but this is the first as a couple.

"Cold?" I ask, noticing her shiver as we get farther out into the ocean. This time of year, the wind can be freezing on the water, but I came prepared.

"A bit, someone didn't tell me what we were doing," she teases, nudging me in the arm with her elbow.

I pull a gray plush blanket out of the bag I packed and brought with us.

"Here." I cover her shoulders and lead her to a covered area of the deck that has a table set for our lunch. "Let's sit."

"Honestly, Griffin. This is too much." She's staring out onto the water from the side of the boat, mesmerized.

"Whoever convinced you that there was a cap on someone doing special things for you was wrong. It will never be enough, and I'll spend all the rest of your birthdays showing you how amazing I think you are."

"Wow," she says quietly, turning to look back at me.

"Wow what?" I run my hands up and down her blanket covered arms.

"You're better than any book boyfriend ever," she tells me before leaning over to kiss me. "Thank you."

"No thanks needed. And of course, I'm better than a book boyfriend," I explain. "I'm real. And I plan on showing you how real I am later tonight. But first, lunch."

As soon as we finish talking, the boat captain shows up with his crew member who's holding a tray with the best-looking lunch I could imagine. We eat our stuffed tilapia, potatoes, asparagus, and homemade bread slowly while we discuss everything in our lives. The two of us have never had a problem talking. She doesn't shy away from me like she does others.

We spend the rest of the afternoon on the water relaxing before we head back to Scott's Bay to meet up with everyone else for cake and hanging outside by the fire pit in my yard.

We don't make it to my bed until almost midnight. Not that I'm complaining. Any night I get to be with her is a great night especially if that night ends up with us both naked.

I wake early the next morning to go for a run before work. Leni's still asleep, so I crawl out of bed and get dressed as quietly as I can. I don't have to work until later in the day, but she has to be at the library in a couple of hours.

I'm halfway done with the run and about to turn to head home when I notice Jack sitting outside the café alone. It's barely eight in the morning, so I'm surprised he's up and out already.

I jog across the empty street to the café but before I can get there, I see a man in a suit come out the doors and sit down at the table with him. Not wanting to interrupt, I quickly turn around and head back home, making a mental note to ask him how things are going. I know it's been a rough few months and I don't think things are great between him and Shelby right now.

I smell the coffee brewing immediately upon opening the front door. Expecting Leni to already be showered and dressed for work I'm surprised to see her sitting at the table in just my station T-shirt.

Surprised, but not upset. Her in my shirt is still the hottest fucking thing in the world.

"Well, hey there," I greet her as I head into the kitchen to kiss her good morning. "Get up late?"

"No, but I realized that it's Sunday and technically I can go in a bit late today since we don't open until noon. I might get stuck there late, but it's a sacrifice worth making if it means I can shower with you after your run."

"Yeah?" I pull my sweat-drenched T-shirt over my head right in the middle of the kitchen, discarding it on the floor.

"Not going to give up the opportunity to clean you up after you got all sweaty. When I realized where you were this morning, I went ahead and checked my schedule to make sure no one else was coming in."

"I'm not complaining at all," I tell her as I grab her hand and lead her back toward the master shower. By the time I have the hot water running, she's already pulling the shirt over her head. To my complete surprise, she isn't wearing anything underneath.

"Well, I've been thinking about this for a while," she tells me, stepping into the shower under the hot water.

"We've showered together before," I tell her, confused but still very much happy to be here with her.

"Not what I'm thinking," she informs me before closing the curtain to wait for me to join her.

"Holy shit," I whisper to myself in anticipation.

CHAPTER 24

Leni

I'M NERVOUS. I'VE NEVER DONE THIS BEFORE. I'VE HAD A FEW boyfriends. I'm not a virgin or anything, but I've never in my life been compelled to go down on a guy. It just wasn't something I wanted to do and since I've only ever dated shy nerdy types no one has ever brought it up.

The more time I'm with Griffin intimately the more I want to try anything and everything we're both comfortable with. When I woke this morning and he was gone my mind started to wander to all the things we've done together, and I started to think about the things we haven't yet done.

He walked into the kitchen after his run and his pheromones hit me. I realized right then just how desperate I am for his taste and to see him go completely off. I want a front-row seat to the best show around and I plan on getting it today.

Once he joins me in the shower we take our time making sure the other is clean. After several minutes of kissing under the hot spray, I slide down his slick body until my knees hit the shower floor.

I look up at him and my eyes lock with his hazel ones. They're full of desire and lust and I see a spark run through them as I tie my long wet hair up in a messy bun on top of my head.

Somehow at the same moment in time, I feel more like myself than

I ever have and like someone completely different. I'm excited and nervous but not hesitant.

Griffin is completely silent, watching my every move. I can feel the excitement in the air as I lift up on my knees and take him in my fist, never breaking eye contact while the hot water flows down my back.

"You're so hard," I whisper as I gently guide my hand up and down. "Wow."

"Fuck," he moans, closing his eyes, his back leaning against the wall under the showerhead. "Leni, if you keep doing that, I'm gonna come."

"You could come just from this?" I say, looking down at my hand stroking him.

"Pretty sure I could come from just looking at you on your knees in front of me," he says through gritted teeth.

I decide right then and there that that's not what I want. I want to see him come. I want to taste it. I want to be the wanton girl who gets to live the dream and not just fantasize about it alone in bed.

I'm mesmerized by the beautiful sight of the enormous cock in front of me. Also slightly scared. No way is that fitting anywhere inside my mouth.

"It's okay, Leni, just please touch me. You don't have to do anything you aren't ready for."

He thinks I'm not ready. I've been fucking ready for this day for years. Grabbing the base, I waste no time in taking the head of it in my mouth. I hear his breathing increase and I'm loving how much power I have right now. Me, Evangeline Hughes, is making Griffin lose control and I love it.

Slowly, I start moving the hand I have at his base up and down him as my lips lather attention on his tip. I can't go very far down yet, but he doesn't seem to mind. I'm so lost in the idea that I'm actually touching him like this I almost miss his hushed cry.

"Faster, please, Leni, faster." He's pleading with me and I love it.

I pause just for a second to look up at him, his cock still filling my mouth. He's staring down at me, water dripping down his head. He doesn't seem to mind. Seconds later I go back to giving his cock all my attention.

I don't hesitate a moment longer. I start bobbing my head up and down, working my hand in unison. I'm desperate for him to finish to show myself I can do this. I can be in control.

It doesn't take long before I taste the salty release. I slow, not wanting to miss a second of his reaction. I watch the ecstasy take over his face as I swallow down every drop. Wiping my mouth, I stand, ready to back away.

"That was the hottest thing I've ever done," I say out loud but just to myself.

"Maybe so far, but I have big plans," he tells me, a hungry look in his eyes.

"I didn't do that expecting anything in return," I inform him, my back up against the wall as I work to steady my rapid breathing.

"I know, sweetness," he says, stepping closer, moving into my personal space. "But if you think I'm not already ready for more, then you are vastly mistaken. Do you know how many nights I jerked off to the thought of what just happened?"

I shake my head, a small smile on my lips as we both get out of the shower and he wraps a towel around me before putting one around his own waist.

"Too many to ever count," he tells me with a chuckle. "But I have to be honest, Leni." He pauses to kiss my lips. The same lips that were just wrapped around his cock moments ago. "Reality is a million times better than my imagination."

"Yeah?" I ask bashfully, just wanting to hear him say it again.

"Definitely," he reassures me as he leans in to kiss the side of my neck. Nothing but towels separate us.

"I have to go," I tell him as I pull back out of his touch. "I'm already late." If I don't leave now I know I'll end up calling in sick and exploring his whole body all day long.

"I know. I love you."

"I love you too."

These past few months with Griffin have been perfection. I never knew life could be this amazing and yet here I am living my dream.

Tomorrow is supposed to be sunny, so I've invited Parker and Mikaela to spend the day with me and Nan. Griffin is working and then said he's going to hang with Jack, who's having a hard time lately.

Every year when the weather gets nice Nan and I head out to the local flea market on Saturdays. She loves to search for treasure, and I like to see if I can find antique books at a good price.

Usually, we both end up coming home with some sort of retro and possibly bedazzled outfits, not to mention the million tea floral teacups we've collected. Neither of us even really drinks tea.

We all pile into my small old car. She's not pretty, but she gets the job done.

"Not to be ungrateful for being invited out today, but you know it's eight-thirty in the morning, right?" Parker asks from the back seat. Based off the fact that they are both rubbing their eyes and yawning every few minutes since we got together, I don't think they are early risers.

Nan and I like to sleep in, but not quite as much as we love looking through other people's junk.

"All the good stuff will be gone by ten. As is, we are running late. We should've been there by seven," Nan explains while I drive.

She's been doing so much better, even walking without her walker some, though secretly I think she enjoys having a compartment to put things in. Last week I caught her pulling an entire bottle of wine out of it while we were walking around the neighborhood, taking a swig and putting the screw cap back on.

By nine we've parked and are already on the hunt for treasure. We're all sticking close together, but we do end up spreading out over a few stalls. I'm searching through an old box of books, looking to see if there is anything I'd like to add to my collection.

"Oh oh oh!" I hear Mikaela squeal from just a few spots down. "I need this."

"Shh, girl!" Nan yells to her as she makes her way over to her. "Don't let on you like something."

Not seeing anything I want, I head over to them, Parker on my heels. I get there just in time to hear Nan teaching her the important rules of bartering.

"You gotta act like you're doing them a favor by taking it off their hands," she's quietly explaining. "I swear once I had someone pay me to take an old table off their hands. Gave it a coat of paint and it's currently in our kitchen."

I just shake my head, knowing how much she's exaggerating, but I let Mikaela have the same fantasy I had of Nan as a child. That she's magical and can do anything.

"Now, what is it, child, you just have to have?" Nan finally gets around to asking her.

"This!" She excitedly holds up an old worn-out American Girl doll. The hair is cut up and the clothes stained. But these dolls are always a hot commodity, so the price tag on it is fifteen dollars.

"I've always wanted one, but they are so expensive, and Daddy always said no."

I look at Parker and see the pain on her face. I don't know a lot about Mikaela's life before Parker got her, but I know that since she moved in with her, Parker has worked hard to provide for them. But money is tight and fifteen on one doll is still a lot.

I'm just about to speak up and offer to pay for it, as they have both done so much for Nan and me over the last several months, but I don't even get a chance.

"I'll take care of this." Nan grabs the doll out of Mikaela's hands and barges over to the person running the stall.

The three of us watch in amazement as she begins a heated round of bargaining. I can't hear anything, but the way she's pointing to the stains on the outfit and where the hair has clearly been cut I know she's giving them hell.

"She's something else, isn't she," Parker says beside me.

"Always has been," I reply, still watching them go at it.

"She doesn't give up, does she?" she asks just as I see Nan open her wallet and throw some bills down in the man's hand.

"Not until she gets what she wants, and I don't just mean when shopping."

"Here you go, baby girl," Nan says before handing Mikaela the doll as well as a small bag of doll clothes.

"What do I owe you?" Parker asks while rummaging through her purse.

"You don't owe me anything," Nan informs her. "You, however"—she points to Mikaela—"you owe me five dollars' worth of chores this week."

Mikaela just nods, already looking through the bag of doll clothes.

"Sure thing, whatever you need. Think you can add a dollar onto those chores and spot me for a hot chocolate?"

"Mikaela!" Parker yells out, horrified.

"Sure thing, child! Let's go get one, sounds good to me." Nan ignores Parker's cries and leads Mikaela away with her.

The two of us continue to walk around, browsing through stuff. Neither of us buys anything, but we're just enjoying each other's company. She's in the middle of telling me how she wants to open her own shop one day when my phone rings and it's a number I don't recognize.

I hit ignore, not wanting to be rude, but not two minutes later it rings again. Parker is so excited telling me about her future plans that once again she doesn't notice, so for the second time I hit ignore, positive it's just a telemarketer or something.

But five minutes later when the same number shows up for the third time, I know something's wrong. I stop dead in my tracks and answer.

"Hello?" I answer, my voice already trembling.

"Leni," a male voice says on the other end of the line. His voice is full of worry and panic. A huge pit forms in the bottom of my stomach. This isn't right. I just know it. "Leni, it's Jack. Where are you? I've gone to the library and your place."

I don't move. I don't talk. It takes everything in me not to drop the phone. Something terrible has happened to Griffin. There's no other reason why Jack would so frantically be looking for me.

"What's wrong? What happened to him?" I finally ask. Parker's still talking a few feet ahead of me, but once I utter those words she stops and slowly turns around.

"There was a fire in the next county over, big one. At a warehouse," he starts to tell me, and I feel my legs get weak. Luckily, Parker notices something is wrong and, in an instant, she's there holding me up by my elbow.

"Where is he?" I need to get to him. "Is he . . ." I can't say the words.

"County hospital. He's alive and stable. A beam fell and trapped him inside. His gear worked, but the beam landed on his leg. We got to him as soon as we could. He was trapped for twenty minutes. His air ran out and he took in smoke. He was unconscious when we got to him." I'm already rummaging through my purse for my keys.

"How is he?" I ask, my voice small as I hold back the tears that desperately want to fall.

"Stable," he repeats his earlier statement. "But I know he wants you there. You're all he talks about. He loves you."

"Oh, yeah, umm, of course. I'll be there as fast as I can." I hang up the phone and just stand in the middle of the flea market. I can't lose him. I know this was a possibility, but I tricked myself into thinking that if I loved him enough, he'd stay safe.

Everyone I love gets hurt or dies. I'm bad luck. Frozen, images of my mom sick in her recliner chair and one of Nan passed out on her bedroom floor flood my mind.

"Go," Parker says, snapping me out of my inner turmoil.

"I can't just leave y'all here."

"Hush," she says. "Your man needs you right now. I'll get Helen to call that man of hers to come pick us up."

"Okay, yeah. Please tell Nan what's going on. I'll call y'all when I know more."

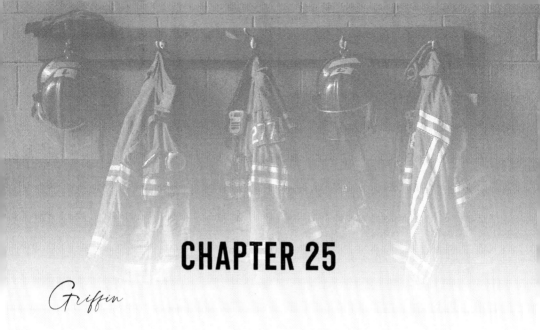

CHAPTER 25

Griffin

MY EYES ARE HEAVY, BUT I'M DETERMINED TO OPEN THEM. I blink them open a couple of times, but each time they close immediately. I feel a hand grab mine and I know it's her.

She's here. It's going to be okay.

"Hi." I hear her soft voice in my ear. "Wake up, please. Please wake up."

I cough as my eyes fully open and the first thing I see is her sitting in the chair holding my hand with her head lying on the edge of the bed. She looks utterly defeated.

Shit.

"Hi, babe," I say hoarsely, thankful I'm not intubated. "It's okay. I'm here."

"Griffin!" she yells out. "Thank God. I thought I was going to lose you."

"You can't lose me. I'll never leave you." Her expression is full of stress and pain.

We don't have time to talk before nurses and doctors start taking over. The room stays busy for the next three days, but she never leaves. Even when my parents drove up from Florida, she didn't leave and go home to rest.

No, she insisted they stay at my place and she stayed here. But still, I know things aren't right. While she's been caring, attentive, and physically here, emotionally, she's not here. She's freaked out and I don't blame her. I wish it stopped there.

The first day she was so thankful that I was awake that she was constantly kissing my head and telling me she loves me. As the shock wore off the 'I love yous' became fewer and farther between.

I tried not to overthink it, but all day today if I try to kiss her or tell her how I feel she finds an excuse to leave the room. She tells me she needs to talk to the nurse or that she's hungry and running to the cafeteria.

"You almost ready?" Leni asks as I put on my shoes. I just changed out of the hospital gown and into some clothes my parents brought me. They came by this morning before heading back to their house in Florida. They offered to stay longer, but after all the hustle and bustle of the hospital, I'm more than ready for some peace and quiet at my place.

"I'm more than ready to get out of here," I tell her with my best attempt at sounding cheerful. I was lucky enough that my gear did what it was supposed to do and kept me safe. My lungs need a week or so to heal fully but other than some bumps and bruises I'll be fine.

"Great, I'll tell the nurse to bring in the wheelchair." She picks up the bag with her stuff in it and the bag with the few things I have.

"I don't need a chair," I tell her. "I can walk."

"It's policy," she says what I honestly already know. "I remember from when Nan was here."

Fifteen minutes later I'm in the passenger seat of her car on the ride back to my place. She isn't talking, but I'm not gonna let her shy away from me. We pull into her driveway.

I'm just about to get out of her car when I hear the words I've been dreading.

"We need to talk."

"Don't do this, Leni," I plead. I know she's about to run. "Do not do this to us. We do not deserve this." Even though I know what's coming, I stay. I sit in the car and wait for her to try to ruin everything we've built.

"I can't do this, Griffin," she eventually says, her voice weak and tears falling down both her cheeks. "I can't fall for you, love you, build a life with you, and then just lose you."

My heart drops.

"Don't do this, Leni," I beg even though I can tell she's already made up her mind. "Don't give up on the chance for something amazing because of fear. I'm not dead. I'm here and I will be for a long time."

"You can't guarantee that. You can't promise me you won't go to work next week and die on the next call you go on. I can't fall even more for you then worry every night that you won't come home."

"Dammit, Leni." I start to lose my cool, something I rarely ever do. I pride myself on staying calm in stressful situations. "Anything could happen to anyone. You can't live in fear."

"Yes, but you are at a higher risk. And bad things happen to the people I love most. I will not let that happen to you."

"No!" I yell out. I don't think I've ever yelled around her before and the shocked look on her face reaffirms she was not expecting that from me. But this is bullshit. "You aren't doing this to us."

"I just need some time. Please understand that. I know I'm an awful person. I don't like being like this, but I don't know how to just turn the constant fear off. I understand that this will probably make you hate me, but I can't take the chance that I'll fall more in love with you than I already am and then just lose you. It would shatter me. I couldn't come back from that."

I sit, silent. Trying to get my anger under control. She's running from me, from love, from life.

"I'm bad luck. And in your job, you can't afford bad luck," she tells me as if that makes a damn bit of difference to me.

"People get hurt every day!" I yell out while looking out the window. I work hard at staying calm under pressure, but this just hurts too much. "This has nothing to do with my job and everything to do with you being scared of moving forward in life."

"Harsh, Griffin," she says quietly, her head looking out the window.

"It needs to be said. You can't just run away scared of everything difficult in life. You've been dealt a rough hand, but life can still be beautiful. Please stop letting fear get in the way of living your best life." I need for her to understand that these feelings won't go away just because we stop sleeping together.

"I'm so sorry. I hope you forgive me. I can't lose you completely. I hope you still want to be my friend. I need you in my life."

I want to yell at her and tell her that she can't take my heart and then just give it back in pieces and expect a Band-Aid to hold it together. I want to tell her that if I can't have all of her I can't look at her every day as a friend and nothing more. I want to tell her all of that and so many other things. But I don't.

"You're never going to lose me. I made you that promise when things started. But if you're going to give up on something amazing this easily, then I'm going to need some time too. I can't turn my feelings for you off overnight."

"Okay," she says, finally looking at me, her eyes puffy and her cheeks red. I want to take her in my arms and tell her I can fix it. But I can't fix it. She needs to fix it in order for us to work.

"You know when I made the promise to you that no matter what you'd never lose me?" I ask, holding my own tears in, determined to be strong right now.

She just nods but at least she doesn't look away.

"I need you to make me a promise now. Can you do that for me?"

"I can try," she says honestly.

"I need you to promise you'll find someone to talk to. Someone who can help you heal through the pain and loss you've been dealt. Use this time while you figure out what you want to really get some help. You've held all this pain in for so long since you lost your mom. You need to work through that."

Her eyes close, taking in what I'm saying. I'm just happy that she's listening and contemplating what I'm suggesting.

"I'm always here to listen to you and help you as much as I can," I continue. "But, and I say this with only love for you, I really think you need help from someone trained in dealing with grief and loss."

In hindsight, she probably should have talked to a therapist when she lost her mom, but on the outside, she seemed like she was dealing as well as anyone could expect. The two of us started to hang out and Nan probably honestly thought she was healing. It wasn't until more recently that Leni let it show how much she was traumatized by the death.

She's silent for a few seconds before she finally speaks up. "I promise."

"Thank you, and I promise when you are ready for me, either as a friend"—I pause—"or more, I will be here waiting. I will wait forever if it means I might get you."

The words pain me to say. We had it all and in a moment, I lost everything. But I mean it. I'll be here when she's ready.

I don't wait for her to say anything else. I know as hard as this moment is on me it's only going to be harder on her as it all settles, and she has to finally deal with the lingering issues she's built up over the years.

CHAPTER 26

Leni

I HAVEN'T READ A BOOK IN THE WEEK SINCE I WATCHED GRIFFIN climb out of my car and walk into his house. I broke his heart and mine, and I'm not sure I can ever be fixed.

Nan's tried to talk to me several times, even attempted to trick me into seeing him by asking me to go get something outside at the exact moment he'd pull into his driveway. But I keep my distance and stay quiet. Saying the words out loud will just make it all harder and more real.

"Leni? You around?" Parker yells, walking into my house. "I know you're here. I see your car outside."

"In here," I call out from my bed where I'm buried deep beneath a pile of blankets. Other than going to work and when I need to eat this is where I'm spending the majority of my time.

"Up you go," she says, yanking the burrito blanket off the top of me. Yes, it's a blanket made to look just like a tortilla. "No more of this."

"Shoo," I tell her, pulling the next layer of blankets up over my head. Joke's on her, I have an endless supply and no desire to leave this bed. I don't deserve to do anything or have a good day.

"Nope, you, my dear, have an appointment today," she reminds me, not that I've forgotten.

"I know. But hear me out. What if instead of seeing a therapist I just go back to sleep for the next week or so?"

Parker sits on the side of my bed and pulls the blanket from over my face. "It's scary, I know. But what do you want most in life?"

"Griffin," I whisper. "But I don't know if I'll ever be healed enough to deserve him."

"You do know that he loves you as you are," she tells me, and I know she's right.

"I know," I mumble. "But I don't love me as I am," I say reluctantly, knowing I'm talking myself in a circle.

"And that's why . . ." She's smiling at me, waiting patiently.

"That's why I have to take a shower and get dressed so I can go to my first therapy appointment."

"Yay!" she cheers while actually applauding. "I'll be in the living room watching your cable TV. I haven't seen a daytime talk show in for-ev-er."

Forty minutes later I'm showered and dressed, and Parker has a cup of coffee and some toast ready for me. I don't know what I'd do without her right now. When I went to her place after Griffin left my car, I was a crying ball of emotions. She jumped into action and helped me find a therapist here in Scott's Bay.

This is something I know I've needed for a long time, but talking openly about my mom's death, not to mention the fact I've never known my dad is something I haven't been ready to do. Until now.

It wasn't until Nan got hurt and then Griffin's accident that I realized how much my past was holding me back.

Two hours later my first session is over and while I realize there is no miracle cure, I feel relief knowing that there is a plan in place. After talking with Dr. Collins and explaining the severity of everything going on in my life right now, he agreed to see me twice a week initially and then we'll move back to once a week then biweekly as I feel improvement.

We've just barely touched the surface of everything that has happened in my childhood, so I know it's going to be a while until I even get around to discussing my relationship or lack thereof. It's going to be a slow process but one that I finally agree has to be done.

I just finished my second session and even though a ton of emotions came up today, more so than during my initial appointment I'm surprisingly in a good mood. Today is the first day in over a week that I want to get out of my house and do something.

After wandering through my favorite used bookstore, I head over to the diner where Parker works. I remember her telling me that she is on the morning shift today so that she could be home when Mikaela gets off the bus.

It's almost the end of March and today is the last day of school before spring break. I thought we could go pick up some pizza and celebrate with Mikaela and Nan the beginning of the break.

The moment I walk through the door to the diner I see him. His back is to me as he sits in a booth across from Jack, but it's Griffin. I'd recognize his dirty-blond hair and tall, muscular build anywhere.

I turn to leave, not ready to see him. Despite living next door to him and working just doors down from him I've managed to avoid having to actually see him. I know that if his hazel eyes meet mine I'll melt.

We've never gone this long without talking and I miss him. Part of me is gone, and without him in my life no amount of therapy can fix it.

I'm still standing here looking at the back of his head when Jack looks up and makes eye contact with me. Slowly, I shake my head from side to side, praying he understands I can't see Griffin right now. Not here. Not like this.

Before he can say anything to Griffin I turn and walk out of the diner. The good mood I was in just moments earlier is fading away quickly. Driving home, I try to remember some of the techniques we talked about in the appointment earlier to deal with disappointment and anxiety.

My initial response was to jump back into bed and hide away for as long as I can. But that's not healthy and it's not going to help.

Instead, I decide upon sitting down and writing my thoughts down on paper. I don't plan on doing anything with it but just getting some of the words out instantly makes me feel better.

Griffin,

I miss you. There, I said it. Not that I think it's a secret because you are my best friend and honestly, I love you. I saw you today. I should have probably said hello or at least asked how you are doing. I made you promise to still be my friend and then at the first opportunity I have to talk to you I run scared. Typical me, am I right? All jokes aside, I miss talking to you more than anything else. No one can replace having you around. I hope you are doing okay. I hope this time apart is treating you well. I hope one day I can work my way back to us. But for now, I just hope that we are still friends.

Love, Leni

Once I finish writing the letter, I go to put it in my desk drawer, not intending to do anything with it. Getting my feelings out really did help. I leave it there and for the first time in too long I pick up a book. It's a romantic comedy and quickly I get lost in the fictional world where a sassy girl gets the cute boy.

Two hours later I've finished half of it and if my stomach wasn't rumbling, I probably would have kept going. I make myself a salad and take it out to sit on the front porch, enjoying the spring weather as the sun sets. I'm sitting here eating my Caesar salad looking over at Griffin's yard. He must still be at work because his truck is nowhere to be seen.

I spend too long lost in my thoughts just looking over in the direction of his house before my eyes catch a glimpse of the little red mailbox. The one in his yard he made for us to pass messages to each other. When I wrote the letter to him, I planned on keeping it secret. Just something I needed to do in order to move forward. But seeing the box with the flag pulled down sparked something inside me.

I want him to read it. Assuming he'll see the lever pulled up and assuming he actually wants to read it. I want him to know what I'm thinking and that I'm working on myself like I promised him I would.

I stand up and walk back into my room and retrieve the letter from my desk drawer. With a determination I'm not used to, I walk barefoot through the house and yard to put it inside his homemade mailbox and raise the wooden flag.

Feeling more relief than I thought I would, I head back inside and allow myself to cuddle up in my bed and get lost back in the sweet book I'm reading, ready to see these two work through their problems to get their happy ever after.

CHAPTER 27

Griffin

I T'S SIX IN THE MORNING WHEN I FINALLY PULL INTO MY driveway. I've been pulling extra shifts all week to avoid being home as much as I can. But after a twenty-four-hour shift, I'm desperate for my bed.

I see it the moment I turn the headlights off. It's still fairly dark out, but the painted red piece of wood on the homemade box sitting next to my house is the first thing I see. Physically I'm exhausted, but the moment I saw that flag pointed upward, mentally I was wide awake.

I walk straight to it and pull it out and put it in my pocket. I thought about just reading it there outside by the floodlights. But I decide I want to sit down and take in what she has to say.

We haven't talked since that awful day. Every second that first week that I thought about her it would feel like someone was stabbing me in the heart. I was home alone for two days before I went back to work and they were the worst days of my life. I haven't even slept in my own bed, opting instead to sleep in the cluttered guest bedroom. There were just too many memories in there.

Just seeing the rumpled sheets lying there where we last left them was torture. After a week I finally washed them but instead of remaking my bed I shoved them all in the hall closet and left the mattress bare.

Even though I'm completely worn out, I have to read the letter. I miss her words, her mind, her heart. I miss everything about her. I've had to stay busy, so I don't run to her. But she says she needs space and time and if that's what she needs, then I will give it to her.

But still, the fact that I haven't heard from her at all has hurt. I get a glass of water and sit down on the couch, letter in hand. Taking a deep breath, I open it and read the words that poured from her heart.

Thirty minutes later I should be going to bed but instead, I'm sitting down at the kitchen table with a legal pad. I think about everything I would have said to her if I knew she was there at the diner. I think about all the thoughts that've been taking over my brain since that day in the car and I pour my heart out to her.

Leni my love,

Thank you for my letter. I've heard that you're seeing someone who can help you. Knowing that has brought the first smile to my face in a long time. I wish you had come and said hi at the diner. I miss your voice. I dream about it every night. I was there with Jack on break. He's having a hard time, so it's been good to talk to him. I hope you are doing well. You have to know that no matter what, we will always be best friends. I can't live without you. But I really do hope that when you are ready, we can be more again. Until then, let's start small. How are you? How is Nan? Update me. I hate not knowing what's going on in your life.

Yours forever,

Griffin

I'm not eloquent or a man who knows a lot of fancy words, but every bit I write comes from the heart. The sun is fully up by the time I place it in the box in her yard and put the flag up. I head back inside and climb in my bed for the first time. For once instead of being sad by the memories of us in here, I'm begging to dream of them. Because for the first time since coming home from the hospital I really have hope for our future.

Over the next few weeks, we write back and forth every day. I tell her about Jack and Shelby separating and she tells me how she walked in on Helen and Leonard making out on the couch. I don't ask her about her therapy appointments. I only know about them because Nan insists on keeping me up to date. But even though I don't outright ask, I can feel her getting stronger and my heart swells knowing she's coming into her own. We don't meet up and we don't call or text and yet I start to feel closer to her than ever before.

It's midday and I'm on my way to work. I stopped by the florist and ordered some peonies to be delivered to the library. Last night when I was reading Leni's latest letter, she mentioned our future. It was in passing, but she clearly is thinking about when we will be together again. I decided then and there it was time to start wooing my girl back again.

I'm not pressuring her or rushing her. I just want her to understand that we do indeed have a future together and that future is starting today. I'm turning the corner to come into the fire station when I hear her voice in the alleyway beside the building.

Panic fills my body immediately because Leni has the voice of the sweetest, kindest angel. But today, right now, it's stern and scared.

"Back up," she calls out to whoever is with her. "I have mace and I will use it."

"You've been coming on to me for weeks," the man's voice responds. A voice I know too well. One I hate. I've had a bad feeling about Ian from the moment he joined our station. He's a creep.

"No, I haven't. I've told you over and over that I'm with Griffin and even if I wasn't you are the last man on earth I would ever consider dating," she responds just as I turn the corner.

"Heard y'all weren't even together," he tells her, and I see red. "Now come on, give me a chance."

"What the fuck is going on here?" I angrily yell out, storming into the alley. "You are messing with my girl?"

"Naw, man." Ian attempts to play it off. "Your girl came looking for me." Even if I hadn't overheard the conversation, the smirk on his face is enough to set me off.

"That's not what happened," she cries out, sounding desperate for me to believe her. Doesn't she know by now that I trust her completely?

"What can I say, man, she's eager to have me alone in a private place. Just came to let her know I don't do my boys that way. Girls are all just fucking whores."

In the background, I hear Leni frantically going on about how she just met with him to tell him how she isn't interested and to beg him to leave her alone. But I barely hear any of it. I'm so pissed at him all I see is red.

I don't even give him a chance to say one more word about her before my fist is flying through the air. Ian immediately goes down like a pile of bricks.

I hear a small scream come out of her mouth and it snaps me back to reality.

"I'm so sorry, love, so sorry." I attempt to console her with one hand on her shoulder while I examine my red knuckles on the other.

Her arms fly up around my neck and I lay my head atop hers. "Why are you sorry? I should have said something to you. I didn't want to worry or upset you. I thought I could take care of this myself. But it's been months of his increasing harassment."

I kiss the top of her head before I step back and look into her deep green eyes. "You can always come to me. Please always come to me," I tell her. "I need to know you are safe and I can't do that if you don't tell me when something's wrong."

I'm leaning against the brick wall, trying to calm my racing heart. When I hear voices in the distance getting closer, no doubt the other firemen heard her scream. I don't hesitate a second. I take her by the hand and move her back out of the way. Just as I begin to let go, she squeezes my hand and gives me a smile. One like she used to give me every night right before we would go to sleep.

It calms me. I feel my heart rate steadying and I breathe easier.

"I love you," I whisper out without thinking. I haven't said those words out loud to her in too long, and it's been killing me. "You don't need to say anything. I just needed to say it. I've never stopped loving you. I think I've loved you since I met you. I loved you even when I didn't like you."

"God, you're perfect. I don't deserve you," she tells me softly right as Jack and two other guys from the station round the corner. I don't have time to tell her the million reasons why she deserves every good thing in life. I'll have to save it for another time.

Ian starts to come to, moaning on the ground, his hand covering the eye that I punched him in just as the other guys arrive.

"You okay?" Jack asks her as the other guys take in the situation and help Ian up.

"I'm fine, please don't be mad at Griffin. This is all my fault. Being a fireman is his passion and as much as I hate him being in danger the idea of him not being able to do what he loves because of me is even worse. I love Griffin and it would kill me to think I cost him his job. Ian's been harassing me for a while and I asked him to meet me here next to the station to tell him to quit or I was going to tell." She's rambling and I should stop it but all I hear is that she loves me and wants me to be a firefighter.

"Shh, babe," I calmly tell her. "I'll be fine."

She takes a deep breath once she notices none of the guys seem upset with me at all. I don't know one guy in our crew who can stand Ian. He's a jerk and I guarantee no one would miss him if he was gone.

"Pharrell," Matt, one of the older men, says to Ian. "Captain wants to see you inside."

I expect a fight or at least him playing the victim, but he just nods and hobbles toward the front door with Matt right behind him.

"Don't worry, Leni, we got your back," Jack says to her while she still clings to my arm. "Shouldn't tell you this, but we've had several complaints about him recently. You should think about making a statement. Pretty sure Captain is ready to fire him. I radioed him and let him know what we stumbled upon."

"How did you know he was harassing me?" she asks him.

"Saw him down and Griffin's red knuckles. Wouldn't take a detective to figure out what happened. Not to mention Pharrell's reputation. Never once in all my years working with Griffin did I know him to have a violent streak. We call him the gentle lion around here."

Once everyone is gone, I lead Leni back to the library.

"Are you going to be okay?" I ask, feeling awful about leaving her here.

"I am," she assures me. "I really am sorry I didn't tell you. I should have."

"Yes, you should have, but it's fine. I'm just glad nothing bad happened to you. I've got to go to work. I'm sure I'll need to file a report about what happened. Please call me if you need me. I'm just down the street," I tell her, hating that I have to leave.

"I'll be fine."

I nod before I turn to leave and just as I get to the door, she calls out my name.

"Griffin."

I turn to look at her beautiful face.

"I've missed your voice."

"I've missed yours too. Does this mean we can start talking again? Not that I don't love your letters."

With a huge smile, she nods before I turn and leave the library.

CHAPTER 28

Leni

I N THE PAST FEW WEEKS SINCE THE INCIDENT AT THE STATION, Griffin and I have been talking every night that he isn't on duty and he's come to have lunch with me at work at least five times. It's like the good old days.

I'm lying in bed thinking about what to do tomorrow when Nan barges into my room.

"When are you going to grow a pair?" she says as if that makes a damn bit of sense.

"What on earth are you talking about?" I ask, completely confused.

"Stringing that poor boy along while you know good and well that you love him, and he loves you."

"It's not that easy," I start to explain.

"Yes, it is. Just stop pussyfooting around," she tells me. Sometimes I feel like I'm the grandmother and she's the woman in her twenties. "If you think you will be any less torn up if something happened to him just because you aren't in a relationship with him, then you are kidding yourself."

"I know," I say sadly. "I'm getting there. I just want to work on making myself as whole as I can be before I give him a piece of me. I love him and I'm learning to love me too."

Much like she came in she walks back out of the room without any warning and I lie here more confused than ever.

Three days later I get home from work and I'm floored. Someone made a mistake and put a For Sale sign in my front lawn. This can't be right; my grandmother wouldn't sell the only home I've ever known without telling me, would she?

"Nan!" I yell out, walking through the house room to room searching for my meddling, pesky grandmother. "I know you are here. Where are you?"

"I'm right here," she calls out from her bedroom. "What's wrong?"

"Why is there a 'For Sale' sign in the front yard?" I ask angrily from the doorway as I watch in confusion as she puts her stuff in a box.

"Peaches, it's time we move on," she says like this makes any sense at all.

"Is there a reason moving on involves actually moving?" I pull the box off the bed and start to put her stuff back in the drawers where it belongs.

"I'm getting older and I really enjoyed my time at the rehab. Not the whole being hurt part, but the community was so nice. They have an independent living section with apartments, and I put an offer in on one and it was accepted."

What the hell!

"And you didn't think to tell me about this before putting the house up for sale?" I'm annoyed and not trying to hold it in. "Maybe talk with me before making life-changing decisions that affect both of us."

"It was a quick decision. Leonard and I were talking a few days ago and realized that if we pool our resources, we could get an apartment at the senior home together and have money to travel a bit. I always wanted to travel and never had time."

Instantly sadness hits me. I know she never intended to raise a kid again, but when my mom got sick, she never hesitated to give me the best life she could. Growing up with her has been amazing, but she's right, it's time to move on.

"But what am I supposed to do?" I ask quietly, ashamed that at my age I still don't know how to move forward in life.

"Seems to me there is a man not far from here more than eager to have you around." She's calmly repacking the clothes I just put back in her drawers.

"You do know we aren't together right now," I remind her. "We just got back to being friends. I want him, but I don't want to feel l like I'm holding him back because my head isn't screwed all the way on."

"Do I know that you acted like a pussy a few weeks ago and walked out on a man who loves you just because he's a good man serving his community while doing a job he loves? Yes, I am aware of that. But I'm also aware that you've been going to that doctor of yours, writing Griffin letters, calling him every day, and every night I see you looking out the window to see if he's gotten home yet. You love that man and he loves you. You just need to have a conversation with him." She pauses for a minute after seeing the panic on my face. "Or you can get your own place. Either way, it's time, don't you think?"

"Yeah." I look around her room and across the hall to mine. "It's time."

Needing some fresh air, I walk out of the house still in shock. Deep inside I knew I wouldn't live here forever and yet I still always had trouble picturing myself moving out. I'm so deep in my thoughts that I don't even notice Griffin standing next to the 'For Sale' sign in the yard.

"You okay?" he asks as I look down at him from the doorway to the screened in porch. Why does he have to be so handsome? It's hard to think straight when he's nearby.

"Umm . . ." I say, finally snapping out of my Griffin induced haze. "I'm not sure. But I think I will be." The two of us are still figuring things out between us. He's being patient with me while I work with my therapist on moving past my issues. But I wouldn't blame him for worrying that I'll just bail when things get rough. I don't want to be like that, but it's hard for me not to hide when I get scared.

"I'm here for you, you know that, right?" He's still standing by the sign. I take a step off the porch closer to him. I don't want to be that scared girl anymore. I'm finally ready to let go of some of the pain I've been holding in for too long.

"You don't seem as shocked as I am," I say, with a slight grin, after realizing how relaxed he is leaning against my mailbox next to that damn sign.

"Well, to be honest," he says, taking a few steps closer to me. "That would be because Helen called me two days ago to tell me her plans."

Shocked, I take a step backward. "Why would she tell you before me about selling my home?"

"I'm guessing for a couple of reasons, one being that she knew you'd probably need a friend. You do not do well with change." He takes a step closer.

"And two?" I ask, not moving out of his way because he's not wrong.

"Two, because I'm so deeply in love with you and I want you to move in with me." He's standing just feet away from me, but he's not moving anymore.

I say nothing. I have no clue how to respond. It's everything I ever dreamed of, but it's a lot and I'm still scared. According to Dr. Collins, I need to give in to my impulses more. Let my instinctual response lead me before the fear can take over and have me second-guessing. Still, that's so much easier said than done.

"Listen, don't say anything. We can do this however you want, but I want you with me. I want you in my life every day, in my bed every night, and more than anything in the world I want to have a family with you one day." He takes a deep breath before continuing. "I know I said I'd be patient, and you are still working on you. And I will be. But please don't get an apartment and move farther from me. If you need more time, take it. Take it from my guest bedroom. I won't rush you. I just can't stand the idea of not having you close."

I stand here for a minute, taking in his words. He opens his mouth to say something, but I don't give him the chance. I rush at him, throwing my arms around his neck, and kiss him passionately.

He gives in with no resistance and grabs me around the waist without pulling back from our kiss. He holds me as tight as he can, as if he could lose me at any second. By the time I pull back he's in a daze and I'm not far off.

"Whoa," he says quietly, rubbing his lips with his fingertips. "Can't say I was expecting that."

"Yeah, I can't say I was planning on doing that either. But I've been working with the therapist I've been seeing, on not running from what I want because of the fear of losing out."

"Good advice," he says with a smile on his face, still holding me around the waist just a bit more loosely now.

"I wanted to kiss you. I know we've been moving slow, but I wanted to, so I did it. Can't say I regret it."

"Does this mean you'll move in? I promise if you want to stay in the other room, I'll get it cleaned out and decorated just for you. I just want you near me. I love you, Leni. I love you with my whole heart and I'm ready for whatever you need."

"Yes, I'll move in but under one condition," I say, running my hand through the stubble on his cheek.

"What?" he asks reluctantly.

"I'll move in as long as we can get some new bedding for our bed," I say with my best attempt at a sexy grin. "Blue plaid screams bachelor and you are no bachelor."

"Yes! Thank fuck! Anything you want," he says, his voice filled with joy. "Even before I was completely in love with you, you were the only person I wanted to spend time with. But now, after everything, I can't imagine being that close to you every night and not be with you. It would be torture. So, anything you want to do to our house is fine by me."

I don't say anything else as he takes my face in his hands and kisses me like there's no tomorrow. Pulling back, he takes me by the hand and leads me across the yard to his place.

Our place.

Walking through the front door, I stop for a moment and he turns to look at me. For the first time in a long time I feel completely and utterly happy. This is exactly where I'm meant to be and who I'm meant to be with.

"I can't promise I won't get scared every time my phone rings when you're at work. Or that I won't check in on you to make sure you're okay. But I can promise I'll keep working on myself and working toward understanding there are risks in life that are just worth taking."

"I know, babe. I know and I'm ready to hold your hand every step of the way." He's still holding my hand as we walk through the house and straight into the bedroom.

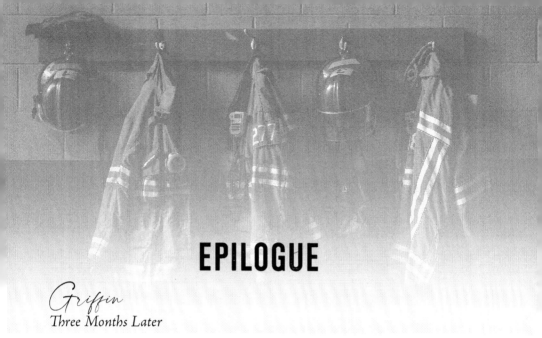

EPILOGUE

Griffin
Three Months Later

"Morning, sunshine." Her soft words coo in my ear. I roll over to see her lying on her side staring down at me.

"You're up early," I tell her.

"Just excited to have today off with you," she says. "What do you want to do today?"

It's been two weeks since our schedules lined up for us to be off together and I don't blame her at all for being excited. I've been desperate to be able to spend a whole day with her and not just a few hours here and there.

"I was thinking we could go shell hunting," I say casually. "It's been a long while since we've done that and I'm in the mood to win a big seafood dinner."

"Good plan. I think when I win, I'm gonna get the steak and lobster dinner."

"Well, bring your wallet because when I win, I'm getting crab legs."

"You're on," she says with a giggle.

An hour later we're walking along the shore, hand in hand. Tourist season has ended, and a lot of the shells have been picked over. Right after summer is never prime shell hunting time, but that's never stopped us before.

"Do you think Toby would mind a dog?"

"You want a dog?" I ask her. "I always thought you were a cat person."

"I am, duh." She nudges me in my side with hers. "But you've always talked about wanting one. I know you've never gotten one because of your hectic schedule and the fact that sometimes you do overnights at the station. But I'm home every night."

I stop walking to turn to look at her. "Could you get more perfect?"

"I dunno, probably," she teases.

Remembering my plan, I start to sweat a bit. I've never been a nervous guy before. It's what makes me a good firefighter. Still, being open and vulnerable with her can be scary. I don't want to do anything to make her freeze up.

"Dibs!" I yell out, pointing to a spot just behind her. "That one's mine!"

"What are you talking about? I didn't see anything." She walks behind me, hands on hips, as I bend down. Just before she gets to me, I pull the shell I've stored in my pants pocket out and drop it onto the sand.

"Cheater!" she yells out, rushing up behind me. "I saw that, Griffin Thorne, you cheat. You aren't getting a dinner out of me."

She's pissed as she walks up to where I'm still bent down, shell in hand.

She's about to start ranting again when she finally gets a good look at me bent on one knee with the shell sitting on my palm facing up.

A gasp escapes her lips when she notices the diamond ring sitting just inside the opening of the shell.

"Griffin," she says as a single tear falls down her cheek. I take her hand in my free one.

"Leni, my love. I think I first fell for you that first day you followed me to the field kicking and pouting. I was just a kid then and couldn't admit that I liked a girl, especially one who was so obviously annoyed by my presence. Then we got older and we got closer and I stopped wanting to hang out with anyone but you. You make my days better. Your smile brightens the darkest days. I meant it when I said I'd wait for you forever. But I'm hoping I won't have to. I'm hoping you'll agree to be my wife and spend the rest of our lives together. I want to grow old with you, I want a dog with you, I want kids with you. I want it all. Please, Leni, will you marry me?"

"Yes! Yes! Yes!" she squeals. "A thousand times yes."

"Really?" I can't help but ask.

"I've never been so sure about anything in my life. I love you so much. I want everything with you too."

Sliding the ring on her finger, I take her in my arms and hold her tight. I knew this felt right to me, but I was still more nervous than I've ever been. I'm tempted to pinch myself to make sure this isn't a dream, but if it is I never want to wake up.

"I love you too," I say, entwining my fingers with hers, my thumb running over the back of the band.

"But you're still buying dinner. Cheating on finding a shell is an automatic forfeit."

"I will get you any dinner you want," I tell her. "But to be fair I did find this shell. Just not today."

"Really?" she asks, her brows furrowed. "When?"

"This was the first shell I ever found when we started this game way back when."

"You kept it?"

"Of course. I think even back then I knew it was something special to hold onto, just like you."

The End.

Enjoy this preview of

Fixing Her

Chapter One

Temperance

"ELEANOR GRACE, GET YOUR CUTE, TINY TUSHY OUT here right this second." I'm rushing through the house yelling out to my menacing little girl, searching every little nook and cranny. With her loose blond curls, hazel eyes, and button nose my daughter might have the face of an angel, but she's as devious as they come. How someone so young is able to plot and carry out plans that are able to alter my entire day is beyond me.

There was no way to prepare for the chaos my life would become after I had a child. At twenty-two, I found out the only one-night stand I'd ever had made a baby. I was twenty-three when I realized I'd be raising this beautiful, special little girl on my own. One day I was single and only having to care for myself and then the next I had this baby, who was depending on me for everything.

It didn't take long before I knew we couldn't survive with me working one job; we'd get by even if it meant constant worries and struggles. I wanted more for her and if that meant me sacrificing, then I would. I'd do anything for her life to be happy.

A little over three years since her birth and we're not only surviving, but thriving together. I often joke that my daughter is an asshole and, trust me, she is, but she's also a blessing. I love being a mom to her and though it's been tough at times, I wouldn't change these last four years since finding out I was pregnant for anything.

Some mornings, though, this being one of them, I wonder how other people got docile, sweet daughters who calmly play with dolls, while I ended up with one whose favorite phrase is "Worry about yourself."

"Ellie, seriously, sweetie! This is not funny. School starts in twenty minutes and if I'm late dropping you off again I'm gonna get in trouble."

I'm desperately looking in every small hiding spot I know of in the house. Holding in my frustration, I continue to plead with the little devil I created.

"Please don't make Mommy sit through a 'We really need all kids here by 9:15 a.m. so we can start the class without any disruptions.' talk again. Please, baby girl."

This is what I'm reduced to, begging a three-year-old to come out of hiding so I can save face. "If we leave now maybe after school we can go out for donuts." Yeah, I'm that mom. Judge me.

A squeaky giggle from my bedroom tells me everything I need to know. I tiptoe into the room and as stealthily as I can I grab the ankles of my girl and tug her out from under my unmade bed. The blankets and sheets that were just seconds earlier piled atop the edge of the bed are now covering her seemingly innocent face.

She continues to giggle as I untangle her and pull her up into my arms. I grab my purse, her tiny backpack, and a hair bow from the table next to the door as I rush out of my small house into the carport where my 2004 brick-red Toyota Camry is parked.

Getting a glimpse of my reflection in the window confirms my fears. The twenty minutes I spent searching for my mischievous daughter would have been better spent using a hairbrush, some concealer, and dressing in something other than sweatpants that are four sizes too big and have elastic in the ankles.

ELASTIC IN THE ANKLES.

Sadly, the ladies at the daycare won't even bat an eye at my outfit or that my hair and makeup are clearly remnants of yesterday's attempt at looking like a human. This is more the norm for me than the put together looks most of the other moms sport first thing in the morning.

I drop Ellie off only six minutes late with the promise of donuts and chocolate milk when I pick her up and somehow even manage to evade Mrs. DeMarco, the woman who runs the Ribbits and Rainbows Learning Center. A miracle in itself since her life goal is to point out what a 'hot mess mom' I appear to be. Like I don't already know. Hello, I own a mirror.

Pulling out of the school's parking lot, I breathe a sigh of relief that I don't have to rush to work. Usually, I have to be at the office immediately after dropping my little girl off. Often I'm running late because of my inability to get my shit together in the mornings. This has been cause for contention with me and my boss over the past three years.

But today Mr. Garcia has a conference out of town, so I can work from home. I'm lucky to have found a job in this town that pays decent. The main downfall, however, is that my boss is constantly a complete ass.

I can't complain. I need this job. Even with the steady income I still need to have several other part-time gigs. The joys of being a single mom are never-ending.

I roll the window down, enjoying the breeze, and decide to treat myself to a coffee from my favorite coffee shop, Brewed. I don't typically splurge on myself, but it's been a crap morning, and I desperately need the dose of caffeine, sugar, and whipped cream that an overpriced coffee drink delivers. Caffeine is a must before I attempt to run into the grocery store for milk unnoticed and then home to tackle the stack of overdue bills just waiting to ruin my rare day off.

I order the most over-the-top sugar-coma inducing drink I can find on the menu and pull through the drive-thru. Coffee in hand and blasting Taylor Swift on the radio, I'm ready to tackle the day. Thank God, I grabbed my oversized sunglasses. Hopefully, I can make it into the store then home without running into anyone I know.

I barely make it to the grocery store before my decision to drive one-handed while using the other hand to drink my much-needed coffee proves to be yet another mistake.

"FUCK!" I cry out as the burn of the hot liquid sears my skin. My loud shriek made everybody in the parking lot stop and look my way. I jump out of my car, hoping to avoid a massive stain on the seat, and just as my feet hit the ground I hear a loud crunch.

Immediately I notice my white T-shirt has now been blessed with a coffee stain all down the front, and I don't even need to look down to know my sunglasses fell off during my leap out and have now been obliterated by my hot pink flip-flops.

"Great, just great," I mumble to myself as I open the back door and search for a jacket, scarf, or anything that might hide the clear display of my klutziness.

Sadly, this was the week I decided cleaning out the car would be a good idea. That'll teach me. Coming all the way back here later with Ellie is not worth the trouble, so I hold my head high and head into the store. I'm about to approach the checkout, grateful I haven't run into anyone I know. Red Oak's a smaller town, and it seems you can't toss a stone without hitting an acquaintance.

Just as I start to think I've got the all clear and will get out of here unnoticed, the ringtone for my best friend, Leigh Ann Simms, "Baby Got Back" by Sir Mix-A-Lot, starts playing at full volume from inside my bag. Seeing as how it's stuffed full of sippy cups, pull-ups, crackers, lollipops, and no less than three dolls, it takes a solid minute before I can wrangle the phone out of its depths to answer it.

"Mouse, where are you right now?" Leigh whispers through the phone. Leigh and I have been inseparable from the day she moved to town in the second grade. We could not be more different, but some-how our friendship just works.

"Store," I respond. "Had to grab Ellie some milk. I desperately need her to go to bed at a reasonable time tonight. Was out of it last night and it took over an hour to convince her she didn't have to have it before going to sleep. Not gonna let that happen again."

"Good. You're close. Put it down and drive to my parents'. Stat. There's no time to waste. Get here. NOW. I gotta go." She immediately hangs up the phone, leaving me questioning what could possibly be so important.

I toss the milk at the closest associate and hightail my ass out of the store to my car like it's on fire. Fearing the worst, I speed the half mile to the Simms' house.

I pull into the oddly full driveway, but I'm relieved that none of the cars occupying it are emergency vehicles. Glancing in the mirror, I attempt to clean up the crusty eye makeup currently surrounding both eyes but give up and admit it's a losing battle. Ellie refused to stay in her big girl bed last night and by the time she finally fell asleep, it took every ounce of my energy just to get into my own bed. No way was I wasting a moment of precious sleep to clean my face.

Yeah, kinda regretting that decision right about now, which seems to be the theme of the day. Sighing, I come to the conclusion this day is not going to get any better and make my way out of the car and up the porch stairs. I have my fist in the air ready to knock, but before I can even get the chance, the door is yanked open and Leigh grabs my wrist, dragging me through the front door, down the hall, and into the hall bathroom.

"What in the ever-loving hell is going on?" I whisper, thoroughly confused.

"Really, Temperance, really," Leigh sighs. Frustration and judgment drip through her voice while studying me up and down.

I know I'm not looking my best, but honestly, is now really the time for her to worry about my appearance? She's the one who demanded I get here right away.

"You did not go into the store like that. Please, I'm begging you to tell me you didn't go into the store dressed like that. Please tell me that on the way here you saw a homeless woman, took pity on her, and traded clothes." Her eyes are closed now as she awaits confirmation of what we both know is the truth.

"I just had to run in. I had a hell of a morning and this"—I point up and down my body—"is the result of you thinking it was a good idea to teach Ellie hide and seek. Deal with it."

"I thought I told you that you were never allowed to wear those pants outside of your house. I knew I should have burned them when I had the chance. I don't care how comfy they are, they add at least fifty pounds to you." She begins the lecture I've heard no less than twenty times. I zone out as she lists the many reasons my favorite pants, as well as most of my entire wardrobe, is not acceptable. I've told her I'm not searching for a man, so I don't care if my comfy lounge pants are unattractive.

"Leigh! If I promise to let you burn them next time we have a bonfire, will you tell me why I abandoned my milk and braved being seen by your parents like this? Are they okay? Is someone hurt?" I interrupt her well-practiced rant, needing answers to my million burning questions.

"Okay, don't freak," she starts, but that phrase alone is enough to get my pulse racing and my brain going to every possible worst-case scenario. "Asher Kade is here."

Fixing Her is available now!

OTHER BOOKS

Fixing Her

Fixing Him,

Fixing Us

Miss Apprehended

Miss Understood

ACKNOWLEDGEMENTS

TJ, Trey, Jacob, and Sophie: Everything I do, I do for y'all! I love you with all my heart.

Amie: Thank you for telling me to stop procrastinating and write the damn book.

My Amazing Betas: Renee, Kelly, Megan, Amie, Charlene, and Ebonie. Thank you for having my back and checking my words. Your insights made it possible for me to put out the best book I could.

Thank you to the amazing team with Social Butterfly, PR. I can't imagine putting out a book without you by my side. Each and every release I feel honored you choose to take a chance on me when I was a brand new baby author.

Thank you to my amazing cover designer, Jay Aheer, with Simply Defined Art, for putting the thoughts in my head together into something beautiful.

Thank you to Lindee Robinson for the amazing photo! It's Leni and Griffin come to life.

Amber Goodwin, you are one of the hardest workers I know and I greatly appreciate all you do.

My editor, Emily A. Lawrence, and my proofreader, Julie Deaton, consistently show me I know nothing of grammar and I'm forever impressed with your knowledge and patience with me.

Stacey Blake, with Champagne Book Design, your formatting always adds the special touches to my books, thank you!

Lastly, to the bloggers and readers, I adore you all and I know how much love and effort you put into promoting and sharing the authors and books you enjoy. I just want you to know it doesn't go unnoticed.

ABOUT THE AUTHOR

Miranda is a loving wife and barely surviving mother of three occasionally good kids. Her hobbies include lying to herself about the calories in donuts and banana pudding, as well as running out of excuses when procrastinating. She's been an avid reader since she was a young girl. Whether she's by the pool, curled up in bed, or hiding in the closet, as long as she has a book in her hands she's happy.